# OLD RUSSIAN STORIES BY

# GOGOL

## ILLUSTRATED BY PHILIP EVERGOOD

A PERPETUA BOOK

A. S. Barnes and Company, Inc.

New York

# CONTENTS

# HOW THE TWO IVANS

## QUARRELLED

VAN IVANOVITCH'S winter coat is lovely. Excellent! And what lambskin! Hell, what lambskin! Dove colored by the frost! God knows, I'm sure that its like isn't to be found on anyone else! For Heaven's sake, look at it—especially when he stops to talk to somebody. Look at it from the side! It's simply delicious! You can't describe it. Velvet! Silver! Fire! God Almighty! Holy Saint Nicolas! Why haven't I such a coat? He had it made even before Agafya Feodosyevna started travelling to Kiev. Do you know Agafya Feodosyevna? She's the one who bit off the assessor's ear.

Ivan Ivanovitch is a wonderful man! What a house he owns in Mirgorod! It is completely surrounded by an awning on oak poles and under the awning there are benches everywhere. When it becomes too hot, Ivan Ivanovitch casts aside his fur coat and his underwear and, clad only in his shirt, rests under the awning, watching what takes place in his yard and in the street. And what apple and pear trees grow under his very windows! You only have to open a window—and their branches burst into the room.

9

All this is in front of the house. If you only saw what he has in his garden! What hasn't he? Plums, cherries, wild cherries, various vegetables, sunflowers, cucumbers, melons, pods, even a barn and a smithy.

Ivan Ivanovitch is a wonderful man. He is very fond of melons. They are his favorite dish. As soon as he has finished his lunch and comes out under the awning dressed only in his shirt, he immediately orders Gapka to bring two melons. He cuts them himself, collects the seeds in a separate piece of paper and begins to eat. Then he orders Gapka to bring him an ink-stand and himself, with his own hand, writes an inscription on the paper containing the seeds, "This melon was eaten on such and such a date." If some guest is present at the time, then he writes, "So and so participated."

The deceased judge of Mirgorod always admired Ivan Ivanovitch's house, whenever he looked at it. Yes, the house is not at all too bad. What I like about it is the way the rooms, large and small, are built on to it from all sides, so that if you look at it from a distance, only roofs are visible, planted one on another like a plate of pancakes or a canker of sponge on a tree trunk. By the way, all the roofs are thatched with ordinary rushes. A willow, an oak tree and two apple trees lean on them, using their wide branches as elbows. Among the trees shine smallish windows with carved shutters painted white, which protrude right into the street.

Ivan Ivanovitch is a wonderful man! He is known even to the Commissar from Poltava, Dorosh Tarasovitch Puchivotchka. When travelling from Chorol, he always breaks his journey to stay with Ivan Ivanovitch. And the Arch Presbyter, Father Peter, who lives in Koliberda, always says, whenever approximately five people have joined him, that he has not met anybody who fulfils his Christian duty and who knows how to live as well as does Ivan Ivanovitch.

---

Heavens, how the time flies. More than ten years had already passed since he had become a widower. He had no children. Gapka has children and they often run about in the yard. Ivan Ivanovitch always gives each of them either a cracknel, or a small piece of melon or pear. Gapka keeps the keys of his granaries and cellars. But the key of the large trunk which stands in his bedroom, and of the middle granary, Ivan Ivanovitch keeps himself and does not like anybody to come near them. Gapka is a healthy girl. She wears a blouse and has fresh calves and cheeks.

And what a pious man Ivan Ivanovitch is! Every Sunday he puts on the fur coat and goes to church. As soon as he is inside, Ivan Ivanovitch bows in all directions, usually seats himself in the choir and accompanies the tune very well with his bass. And when the service is finished, nothing can prevent Ivan Ivanovitch from making the round of the beggars. No doubt it is only his inborn goodness that impels him to undertake such a tedious duty.

"Hello, beggar!" he would say, having selected the most crippled woman in a torn dress composed of patches. "Where d'you come from, beggar?"

"I come from the village, Your Honor. It's three days since I've had any food or drink. My own children have driven me out."

"You poor soul! Why, then, have you come here?"

"To beg, Your Honor, for enough money to buy bread."

"Ahem! D'you want some bread then?" Ivan Ivanovitch would usually inquire.

"Yes, sir! I'm as hungry as a dog."

"Ahem!" Ivan Ivanovitch would usually reply. "Perhaps you want some meat as well?"

"Anything Your Honor gives me. I'll be grateful for anything."

"Ahem! Is meat better than bread?"

"Hungry beggars aren't choosers. Anything you give is good."

"Well, go along then, God be with you," Ivan Ivanovitch would say. "What're you waiting for? I'm not beating you, am I?"

And, having made similar inquiries from another and a third, he finally either returns home or drops in for a drink of vodka on his neighbor Ivan Nikiforovitch, or on the judge, or on the provost.

Ivan Ivanovitch likes it very much when somebody gives him a present or some gift. It pleases him enormously.

Ivan Nikiforovitch is also a very good man. His yard borders on Ivan Ivanovitch's yard. They are friends, such as the world has never produced before.

Anton Prokofyevitch Pupopuz, who still wears a brown jacket with light blue sleeves and lunches with the judge on Sundays, used to say that the Devil himself had tied Ivan Nikiforovitch to Ivan Ivanovitch with a string. Where the one goes, the other drags himself, too.

Ivan Nikiforovitch has never been married. They used to say that he had been married, but that is an absolute lie. I know Ivan Nikiforovitch very well and can say that he never even had any intention of marrying. Where does such gossip originate? For example, the rumor was spread at one time that Ivan Nikiforovitch was born with a tail at his back. But that invention is so incongruous and at the same time so base and indecent, that I do not even deem it necessary to repudiate it to my enlightened readers, who, I have no doubt, know that only witches, and very few of them, have a tail at the back. Witches, by the way, tend to belong more to the feminine sex than to the masculine.

Despite their great intimacy, these rare friends were not quite alike. One can best learn to know their characters from comparison. Ivan Ivanovitch possesses the unusual gift of talking extremely pleasantly. My God, how he talks! This sensation can be compared only with the one you feel when somebody looks for something in your hair, or gently presses a finger along your heel. You listen, listen—and hang your head. Agreeable! Amazingly agreeable! Like sleep after a hot bath.

Ivan Nikiforovitch, on the contrary, is more taciturn. On the other hand, if he throws in a word, then just you look out. It will cut you closer than any razor.

Ivan Ivanovitch is thinnish and tall. Ivan Nikiforovitch is slightly smaller, but, on the other hand, he spreads out in width.

Ivan Ivanovitch's head resembles a radish with its tail down. Ivan Nikiforovitch's head resembles a radish with its tail up.

After lunch Ivan Ivanovitch lies under the awning clad only in his shirt, but towards evening he puts on the fur coat and goes somewhere, either to the town store, which he supplies with flour, or into the fields to catch quails.

Ivan Nikiforovitch lies on the porch the whole day—if the day is not too hot. There he usually exhibits his back to the sun—and does not want to go anywhere. If it comes into his head in the morning he will walk across the yard, survey his household and go back again to rest. Formerly he used to drop in on Ivan Ivanovitch.

Ivan Ivanovitch is an extremely refined man and in ordinary conversation will never use an indecorous word and takes immediate offense if he hears one.

Ivan Nikiforovitch will never take enough care. On such occasions Ivan Ivanovitch usually gets up from his seat and says, "That's enough, enough, Ivan Nikiforovitch. It is better for you to leave than to use such ungodly language."

Ivan Ivanovitch gets very angry if he finds a fly in his borshtch. Then he loses his self-control and will smash the plate and the host will suffer.

Ivan Nikiforovitch is very fond of taking a bath. When he is sitting up to his neck in water, he orders a table and a samovar, and loves to drink tea in such coolness.

Ivan Ivanovitch trims his beard twice a week. Ivan Nikiforovitch only once.

Ivan Ivanovitch is extremely curious. God forbid if you begin telling him anything and do not finish it! And if he is displeased with anything, then he immediately shows it.

It is extremely difficult to tell from Ivan Nikiforovitch's expression whether he is pleased or annoyed. Even if he is delighted with anything, he will not show it.

Ivan Ivanovitch's character is somewhat timorous. Whereas Ivan Nikiforovitch's loose trousers possess such wide pleats that, if they were inflated, his whole yard, with its granaries and buildings complete, could be put into them.

Ivan Ivanovitch's eyes are large and expressive and are the color of tobacco, and his mouth somewhat resembles the letter "I." Ivan Nikiforovitch's eyes are small and yellowish and disappear completely between thick eyebrows and plump cheeks, and his nose resembles a ripe plum.

If Ivan Ivanovitch treats you to some tobacco, he will always lick the lid of the snuff-box first, then rap it with his finger, and offering it to you, will say—that is, if you are acquainted with him—"May I, sir, ask you to do me the honor," and, if you are not an acquaintance of his, then he will ask, "Sir, without having the privilege of knowing your rank, name, and surname, may I ask you to do me the honor?"

Ivan Nikiforovitch, on the other hand, puts his pouch straight into your hands and only adds, "Help yourself!"

Ivan Ivanovitch, as well as Ivan Nikiforovitch, strongly dislikes fleas and so neither Ivan Ivanovitch nor Ivan Nikiforovitch will ever allow a Jew to pass with his merchandise, without buying from him various pots of elixirs against such insects, first having scolded him properly for embracing the Jewish religion.

By the way, despite some disparity, both Ivan Ivanovitch and Ivan Nikiforovitch are wonderful people.

## 2

*From which one learns what Ivan Ivanovitch suddenly desired, what conversation*
*took place between Ivan Ivanovitch and Ivan Nikiforovitch*
*and how it ended.*

One morning—in the month of July—Ivan Ivanovitch was lying under the awning. The day was hot, the air dry and transfused with rays of sunlight. Ivan Ivanovitch had already managed to see the reapers outside town and in the village, to inquire from some peasants and peasant women he had met, where they came from, where they were going to and how and why. Having completely tired himself with walking, he lay down to rest. For a long time, lying there, he surveyed the granaries, the yard, the barns and the hens, which ran about the yard, and thought to himself:—

"God Almighty, what a good landowner I am! What is there that I haven't got? Birds, a building, granaries, every luxury, distilled vodka, liquor, pears and plums in the garden, poppy seed, cabbage and peas in the kitchen garden. What else is there that I haven't got . . . I should like to know, what there is that I don't possess?"

Having put such a deep question to himself, Ivan Ivanovitch fell into a reverie and, in the meantime, his eyes found new objects, stepped over the fence into Ivan Nikiforovitch's yard and occupied themselves involuntarily with a curious spectacle.

An emaciated peasant woman was carrying out, one after another, clothes that had long been laid up and was hanging them out to air on a line. Soon an old uniform, with worn cuffs, stretched out its sleeves in the air and embraced a lamé blouse. Behind it peeped out a nobleman's coat with emblem buttons and a moth-eaten collar. Then followed white spotted pantaloons, which a long time ago would have been pulled on Ivan Nikiforovitch's legs and which now could be, perhaps, pulled on his fingers. Soon another pair of pantaloons was suspended, shaped like the letter "H." Then came a blue Cossack jacket, which Ivan Nikiforovitch had had made for himself about twenty years ago, when he was on the verge of entering the militia and had for that reason grown a moustache. Finally, there followed a sword, which, on the line, looked like a spire jutting out into the air. The tails of something resembling a peasant's coat began to whirl, grassy green with brass buttons the size of a five-kopek piece. From behind the tails peeped out a waistcoat mounted with gold braid, cut low in front. The waistcoat was soon covered by a deceased grandmother's old skirt, with pockets, each spacious enough to hold a watermelon. All this hotchpotch presented a very entertaining spectacle to Ivan Ivanovitch, as the sunrays successively seized now a blue, now a green sleeve, or a red cuff or a piece of gold braid. Playing on the sword-spire, they brought memories of a puppet show, presented in the villages by wandering scoundrels, particularly of the moments when the crowd, closely packed, looks at King Herod in his golden crown, or at Anthony leading a goat. Behind the puppet theatre a fiddle squeaks, a gypsy strums on his lips in place of a drum, the sun goes down and the fresh cold of a Southern night imperceptibly presses itself closer to the fresh shoulders and breasts of the plump village girls.

Soon the old woman crept out again from the storeroom and, groaning, dragged an ancient saddle with torn stirrups, worn leather pistol pockets, and a saddle-cloth, formerly red, with golden embroidery and brass plates.

"That's a silly woman," thought Ivan Ivanovitch, "for all I know she might drag Ivan Nikiforovitch himself out for an airing."

And indeed, Ivan Ivanovitch was not far out in his conjecture. About five minutes later Ivan Nikiforovitch's loose nankeen trousers planted themselves in the yard and took up almost half of it. After that the woman brought out a cap and also a gun.

"What does it mean?" thought Ivan Ivanovitch. "I've never known Ivan Nikiforovitch to have a gun! What does he intend to do? He doesn't shoot and yet he has a gun! What does he want with it? And it's a nice piece of work. I wanted to get one myself a long time ago. I'd very much like to have that nice gun. I like toying with a gun. Hey, woman, woman!" shouted Ivan Ivanovitch, beckoning with his finger.

The old woman approached the fence.

"What have you there, granny?"

"You can see for yourself—a gun."

"What sort of a gun?"

"Who knows what kind it is? If it was mine, then perhaps I'd know what it's made of, but it's the master's."

Ivan Ivanovitch got up and began to inspect the gun from all angles and forgot to tell the old woman off for hanging it out to air along with the sword.

"I think it's made of iron," continued the old woman.

"Ahem! Of iron. Why is it made of iron?" Ivan Ivanovitch asked himself. "And has your master had it a long time?"

"May be."

"Nice little thing. I'll ask him to give it to me. What could he do with it? Or I'll exchange it for something. Granny, is the master at home? What?"

-------

"He is."

"Is he lying down?"

"He is."

"All right then, I'll go to him."

Ivan Ivanovitch dressed, took a gnarled stick in his hand, to protect himself against the dogs, for many more of them are encountered in the streets of Mirgorod than people, and left.

Although Ivan Nikiforovitch's yard was near Ivan Ivanovitch's yard, and one could climb from one into the other over the wattle hedge, Ivan Ivanovitch, nevertheless, went by way of the street. From this street one had to cross a side street, which was so narrow that if two one-horse carts happened to meet in it they could not pass, and had to remain in the same position until they were dragged out into the main street in opposite directions by their back wheels. And the pedestrian would adorn himself, as if with flowers, with buds of burdock which grew at both sides of the fence. Into this side street Ivan Ivanovitch's barn jutted out from one side and Ivan Nikiforovitch's granary, gates and dove-cote from the other. Ivan Ivanovitch approached the gates and rattled the latch. Dogs began to bark inside, but, seeing a familiar face, the variegated pack soon ran back wagging their tails. Ivan Ivanovitch crossed the yard which was streaked with multicolored Indian pigeons (usually fed by Ivan Nikiforovitch personally), skins of watermelons and melons and in some places with grass; in other places there would be a broken wheel, or a hoop from a cask or a boy lolling about in a dirtied shirt: a picture which painters love! The shadow of the airing clothes covered almost the whole of the yard and imparted to it some coolness. A peasant woman met him with a bow and remained gaping in the same spot. A porch with an awning on two oak posts preened itself before the house—an unreliable protection against the sun, which at this time in Little Russia does not like joking and floods the pedestrian from head to foot with hot perspiration. How strong was Ivan Ivanovitch's desire to acquire an indispensable object is proved by his decision to go out at such a time and to break his daily rule of going for a stroll only in the evening.

The shutters were closed in the room which Ivan Ivanovitch entered and a ray of sunlight, which pierced a hole in the shutters, assumed a rainbow color and painted on the opposite wall a multicolored picture of thatched roofs, trees, and the clothing hung out in the yard, but all upside down. This created a wonderful semi-darkness in the room.

"God be with you," said Ivan Ivanovitch.

"Oh, hello, Ivan Ivanovitch," answered a voice from a corner of the room.

Only then did Ivan Ivanovitch notice Ivan Nikiforovitch, who was lying on a rug spread out on the floor.

"Forgive me for appearing before you as nature made me"—Ivan Nikiforovitch was lying with nothing on, not even a shirt.

"That's all right. Have you had a rest to-day, Ivan Nikiforovitch?"

"I have. And have you, Ivan Ivanovitch?"

"I have."

"Have you only just got up, then?"

"Have I just got up? For Heaven's sake, Ivan Nikiforovitch! How can one sleep until this time? I've just returned from the village. The corn is wonderful all along the road. Magnificent! And the hay is fully grown, so soft, so smooth."

"Gorpina!" shouted Ivan Nikiforovitch, "bring some vodka and some pies and sour-cream for Ivan Ivanovitch."

"Nice weather we have to-day."

---

"Don't praise it, Ivan Ivanovitch. May the Devil take it! There's no hiding from the heat."

"You would mention the Devil! Listen, Ivan Nikiforovitch. You'll remember what I told you, but it'll be too late. You'll suffer in the next world for blasphemous words."

"Why have I offended you, Ivan Ivanovitch? I didn't refer to your father or your mother. I don't know why I offended you."

"That's enough, now. That'll do, Ivan Nikiforovitch."

"By God, I haven't insulted you, Ivan Ivanovitch?"

"It's strange that quails can't be caught with bird-calls."

"As you wish. Think what you like, but I didn't insult you in any way."

"I don't know why they don't come," Ivan Ivanovitch was saying, as if not listening to Ivan Nikiforovitch. "Perhaps the time isn't ripe yet . . . but it seems that the weather is right."

"You were saying that the corn is good?"

"The corn is magnificent, magnificent!"

Silence followed after this.

"Ivan Nikiforovitch, why are you hanging out your clothes?" Ivan Ivanovitch said at last.

"Because the blasted woman has allowed wonderful, almost new, clothing to rot. Now I'm airing it. The cloth is fine, it's excellent, you merely have to turn it—and it can be worn again."

"I liked one thing there, Ivan Nikiforovitch."

"Which?"

"Tell me, please, what d'you want with the gun, which has been put out to air with the clothes?" Ivan Ivanovitch then offered some tobacco to Ivan Nikiforovitch and said: "May I ask you to do me the honor?"

"That's all right. Have mine. I'd rather have a pinch of my own."

---

Ivan Nikiforovitch felt beside him on the rug and produced his tobacco-pouch.

"What a silly woman! So she's hung the gun out there as well. The Jew from Sorochintsy makes good tobacco. I don't know what he puts into it, it's so fragrant! Tastes somewhat like grass. Take some, please. Chew a little of it. Isn't it like grass? Here you are, help yourself."

"Tell me, please, Ivan Nikiforovitch, I'm still talking about the gun. What will you do with it? After all, you don't need it."

"Why don't I? And supposing I have to shoot?"

"God protect you, Ivan Nikiforovitch. When will you have occasion to shoot? Unless it be at the Second Advent. As far as I know and others remember, you haven't killed a single duck yet, and your nature wasn't designed by God Almighty so that you could shoot. You have the bearing and figure of a weighty man. How can you trail across marshes, when your clothes, which I'm too polite to mention by name, are being aired at this very moment? What? No, you need rest, relaxation." (Ivan Ivanovitch, as has been mentioned above, expressed himself unusually colorfully, when persuasion was imperative. How he talked! My God, how he talked!) "Yes, you should behave decently. Listen, give it to me."

"How can I? It's an expensive gun. You'll not find its like anywhere now. I bought it from a Turk when I intended to join the militia. How can I give it away now, suddenly? How can I? It's an indispensable article."

"Why is it indispensable?"

"What d'you mean, why? Supposing robbers attack the house . . . Of course it's indispensable! God be praised! Now I'm calm and afraid of nobody. And why? because I know that there's a gun standing in my store room."

---

"Is it a good gun? But its lock is spoilt, Ivan Nikiforovitch!"

"What if it is spoilt? It can be mended. You've only to grease it with hemp oil to keep the rust off."

"For the life of me, Ivan Nikiforovitch, I can see no signs of a friendly disposition on your part towards me. You won't do anything for me as a mark of friendship."

"How can you say, Ivan Ivanovitch, that I don't show any signs of my friendship towards you? Aren't you ashamed of yourself? Your oxen graze on my field, and I haven't borrowed them once. When you travel to Poltava, you always ask for my cart. And have I ever refused it? Your boys climb over the wattle hedge into my yard and play with my dogs—I don't say anything. Let them play, so long as they don't touch anything. Let them play!"

"If you won't give it to me, perhaps we could make an exchange?"

"What will you give me for it?" Having said this, Ivan Nikiforovitch propped himself up on his elbow and looked at Ivan Ivanovitch.

"I'll give you the brown pig, the one I've fattened up. It's a nice pig. Next year, you'll see, it'll produce piglets for you."

"How can you make such a suggestion, Ivan Ivanovitch? What good is your pig to me? Unless I use it for a funeral feast in honor of the Devil."

"There you go again! You can't do without the Devil! It's a sin you're committing. By God, it's a sin, Ivan Nikiforovitch."

"What d'you mean, Ivan Ivanovitch? You want to give me in exchange for the gun—the Devil knows what—a pig!"

"Why is a pig 'the Devil knows what,' Ivan Nikiforovitch?"

"And why not? I'd think it over if I were you. A gun—that's a well-known thing, but a pig—is the Devil knows what. If it wasn't you who'd said it, I might have thought it was intended as an insult."

"And what bad things have you noticed about a pig?"

"What do you really take me for? That I should take a pig . . ."

"Sit down, sit down! I'll stop . . . let your gun stay with you, let it rot and get rusty standing in the corner of the store-room. I don't want to talk about it any more."

After that silence ensued.

"They say," began Ivan Ivanovitch, "that three kings have declared war on our Tsar."

"Yes, Peter Feodorovitch told me. What is this war? And why is it on?"

"One can't say for certain why it's on, Ivan Nikiforovitch. I suppose the kings want us all to embrace the Turkish religion."

"So that's what the fools have taken into their heads," said Ivan Nikiforovitch raising his head.

"You see, that's why our Tsar declared war on them. 'No,' he says, 'you'd better embrace the Christian religion.' "

"What of it? We'll beat them anyway, Ivan Ivanovitch."

"We will. So you don't want to exchange the gun, Ivan Nikiforovitch?"

"It seems strange to me, Ivan Ivanovitch, that you, a man with a reputation for learning, should talk like a schoolboy. Am I such a fool . . ."

"Sit down, sit down! Forget it. Let it rot. I shan't talk about it any more."

At that moment the snack was brought in.

Ivan Ivanovitch drank a glass of vodka and took a portion of the pie with some sour cream.

"Listen, Ivan Nikiforovitch. I'll give you two sacks of oats in addition to the pig. You haven't sown any oats yet and you'll have to buy some this year in any case."

———

"By God, Ivan Ivanovitch . . . One should have a stiff drink before talking to you." (That was put comparatively mildly. Ivan Nikiforovitch lets off phrases worse than that.) "Where have you heard of a gun being exchanged for two sacks of oats? I bet you won't give your fur coat for it."

"But you forget, Ivan Nikiforovitch, that I'm giving you a pig as well."

"What! Two sacks of oats and a pig for a gun!"

"What about it? Isn't it enough?"

"For a gun?"

"Of course, for a gun."

"Two sacks for a gun?"

"Two sacks, not empty ones, but filled with oats, and have you forgotten the pig?"

"You can kiss your pig, and if you don't want to, then kiss the Devil!"

"Oh, why are you so quick-tempered? In the next world they'll sew up your tongue with hot needles for such impious words. After a talk with you one has to wash one's face and hands and then one should fumigate oneself."

"Permit me, Ivan Ivanovitch. A gun—that's a noble thing, the finest means of recreation and in addition it's a pleasant ornament in a room . . ."

"Ivan Nikiforovitch, you fuss over your gun like a child over a new toy," said Ivan Ivanovitch with annoyance, as he was becoming really angry.

"And you, Ivan Ivanovitch, behave like a real gander."

If Ivan Nikiforovitch had not said these words, then they would have argued a little with each other, and then, as always, parted good friends. But now things took quite a different turn. Ivan Ivanovitch flared up.

———

*"Take hold of his arms and put him out of the house"*

"What did you say, Ivan Nikiforovitch?" he asked raising his voice.

"I said that you resemble a gander, Ivan Ivanovitch."

"How could you dare, sir, forgetting decency and respect for the rank and the family of a man, to dishonor him with such abuse?"

"What's abusive about it? And why, indeed, have you begun to wave your hands about so much, Ivan Ivanovitch?"

"I repeat, how did you dare, against all propriety, to call me a gander?"

"I snap my fingers at you, Ivan Ivanovitch! Why are you cackling so much?"

Ivan Ivanovitch could no longer control himself. His lips began to tremble. His mouth changed its usual shape of the letter "I" and assumed the shape of the letter "O." He blinked his eyes so much, that it was frightening. This happened very rarely to Ivan Ivanovitch. One had to annoy him very seriously to cause that.

"I should like to inform you," said Ivan Ivanovitch, "that I don't want to know you."

"What a terrible misfortune! By God, I won't weep because of that," answered Ivan Nikiforovitch.

He was lying, lying, by God he was! He was very sorry about it.

"I won't cross your threshold."

"Ehe," said Ivan Nikiforovitch with vexation, not knowing what to do, and against his usual wont, rose to his feet: "Hey, woman, boy!"

At this the same emaciated woman with a smallish boy, entangled in a long wide jacket, appeared at the door.

"Take hold of Ivan Ivanovitch's arms and put him out of the house!"

"What! To do that to a nobleman!" shouted Ivan Ivanovitch with a feeling of dignity and indignation. "You just dare! Try and approach me! I'll annihilate you together with your silly master! A crow won't find your burying place!" Ivan Ivanovitch spoke unusually strongly when his soul was stirred to its depths.

The whole group formed an expressive picture. Ivan Nikiforovitch stood in the middle of the room in all his beauty, absolutely unadorned. The peasant-woman, her mouth agape, bore on her face an expression at once vacant and terror-stricken. Ivan Ivanovitch's hand was raised, in the manner in which we depict Roman tribunes. What an unusual moment! What a wonderful spectacle! But it had an audience of only one. This was the boy in the immeasurable jacket, who stood unmoved and was picking his nose with his finger.

At last Ivan Ivanovitch took up his cap.

"You're behaving very well, Ivan Nikiforovitch! Wonderfully well! I'll remind you of this."

"Get out, Ivan Ivanovitch, get out! And see that I don't come across you. Or else—Ivan Ivanovitch, I'll smash your face in."

"This is what I think of you, Ivan Nikiforovitch," answered Ivan Ivanovitch, snapping his fingers at him and slamming the door, which with a rattle and a yelp opened up again.

Ivan Nikiforovitch appeared in the doorway and wanted to add something, but Ivan Ivanovitch did not turn round and flew from the yard.

3

*What happened after the quarrel of Ivan Ivanovitch with Ivan Nikiforovitch.*

And thus two respectable men, the pride and ornament of Mirgorod, quarrelled with each other! And why? For some absurd reason, because of a gander. They no longer wanted to see each other and severed all connections between themselves. Yet previously they were known as the most inseparable of friends. Every day Ivan Ivanovitch and Ivan Nikiforovitch would send someone to inquire after each other's health, and they would often converse across their balconies and say such pleasant things that it rejoiced one's heart to hear them. On Sundays Ivan Ivanovitch in his fur coat and Ivan Nikiforovitch in a yellowish-brown nankeen Cossack coat would depart together, almost arm in arm, for church. And if Ivan Ivanovitch, who had very good eyesight, was the first to notice in the middle of the street a puddle of some uncleanliness, which is sometimes to be encountered in Mirgorod, he would always say to Ivan Nikiforovitch: "Be careful, put your foot here, for there's something bad there." Ivan Nikiforovitch, on his part, also displayed most touching signs of friendship. However far off he might be standing somewhere, he would always stretch out his hand with the tobacco pouch to Ivan Ivanovitch adding: "Help yourself." And what wonderful households they both had! And these two friends . . . When I heard about it, I was thunderstruck. For a long time I did not want to believe it. God Almighty! Ivan Ivanovitch quarrelling with Ivan Nikiforovitch! Such worthy people! Is there any permanence left in this world?

For a long time after his arrival home Ivan Ivanovitch was greatly agitated. Formerly he would first drop into the stables to see if the mare was eating her straw (Ivan Ivanovitch's mare is a roan with a bald patch on the forehead, a very good little horse), then with his own hands he would feed his turkeys and pigs and only afterwards would he go to his rooms where he either makes wooden dishes (he can produce many things out of wood very skilfully, not worse than a carpenter) or he reads a book printed by Liuby, Gary and Popov (Ivan Ivanovitch does not remember its name, because one of the servant girls tore off the top of the title-page a long time ago, when she was amusing a child) or he rests under the awning. But on this occasion he did not embark on any of his usual occupations. Instead, meeting Gapka, he began to scold her for strolling about doing nothing, although she was dragging a sack of maize into the kitchen. He threw his stick at the cockerel, which came to the porch for its usual offering, and when a dirty boy in a small torn shirt came running up to him shouting: "Daddy, daddy, give me some gingerbread," he threatened him so terrifyingly and stamped so much with his feet, that the frightened child ran away God knows where.

Nevertheless he finally regained his composure and began to occupy himself with the usual matters. He had his lunch very late and did not lie down under the awning till it was almost evening. The good borshtch with pigeons cooked by Gapka, completely drove the morning's incident from his mind. Ivan Ivanovitch again began to survey his possessions with pleasure. Finally his eyes stopped on the neighboring yard and he said to himself: "I haven't been to see Ivan Nikiforovitch to-day. I'll go to him." Having said this, Ivan Ivanovitch took his stick and his cap and departed into the street. But hardly had he stepped out of the gates, when he remembered the quarrel, spat out and turned back. Almost the same procedure occurred in Ivan Nikiforovitch's yard. Ivan Ivanovitch saw that a peasant woman had already put a leg on the wattle hedge with the intention of climbing over into his yard, when suddenly Ivan Nikiforovitch's voice was heard: "Back, back! There's no need for it!"

However, Ivan Ivanovitch became very bored. It was extremely likely that these worthy men would have made peace the very next day, if a special occurrence in Ivan Nikiforovitch's house had not destroyed every hope and poured fat on the fire of enmity which was on the point of dying out.

---

Agafya Fedosyevna arrived at Ivan Nikiforovitch's towards the evening of the same day. Agafya Fedosyevna was neither Ivan Nikiforovitch's blood relative nor his sister-in-law, nor even his godmother. It would appear that there was no earthly reason for her to visit him, and he himself was none too glad to see her. Nevertheless she did visit him and used to stay in his house for weeks on end and sometimes even longer. On these occasions she would take possession of the keys and would take the burden of the household on her shoulders. This was very irksome to Ivan Nikiforovitch, yet, surprisingly, he listened to her like a child, and although he sometimes tried to argue with her, Agafya Fedosyevna always had her way.

I confess, I do not understand why it has been so arranged that women can seize and lead us by the nose as deftly as they manipulate the handle of a teapot. Either their hands have been created for this purpose, or our noses are no good for anything else. And despite the fact that Ivan Nikiforovitch's nose somewhat resembled a plum, she seized him by that organ and by it led him after her like a pet dog. During her stay he even involuntarily changed his usual course of life. He did not spend as much time in the sun as usual, and, if he did, then not as nature made him, but always in his shirt and loose trousers, although Agafya Fedosyevna did not make any such demands. She did not stand on ceremony and when Ivan Nikiforovitch suffered from fever, with her own hands she rubbed him with turpentine and vinegar from head to foot. Agafya Fedosyevna wore a cap on her head, three warts on her nose and a coffee-colored dressing gown with small yellow flowers. Her whole figure resembled a tub, and consequently it was as difficult to find her waist, as to see one's nose without a mirror. Her little feet were short, formed on the pattern of two cushions. She gossiped and ate boiled beetroots in the mornings, and swore extremely well, and during all these diverse activities her face did not change its expression for a moment, an attainment that can be claimed only by women.

As soon as she arrived everything went the wrong way.

"Don't you make peace with him, Ivan Nikiforovitch, and don't you ask his forgiveness. He wants to destroy you. The scoundrel! You don't know him yet!"

The blasted woman whispered, whispered and succeeded well, for Ivan Nikiforovitch did not even want to hear about Ivan Ivanovitch.

Everything assumed a different character. If the neighbor's dog ran sometimes into the yard, it was thrashed with anything in sight. Small boys who climbed over the hedge, returned howling, with their small shirts raised up and marks of flogging on their backs. Even the peasant woman herself, when Ivan Ivanovitch was on the point of asking her a question, made such an indecent gesture, that Ivan Ivanovitch, who was an extremely refined man, spat out and only said: "What a rotten woman! Worse than her master!"

Finally, to crown all the insults, the odious neighbor built right in front of him, on the spot formerly used as a stile for climbing over the wattle hedge, a shed for geese, as if with the special intention of redoubling the abuse. This enclosure, so repugnant to Ivan Ivanovitch, was built with devilish speed—in one day.

This roused Ivan Ivanovitch's spite and the desire for revenge. However, he did not show any outward signs of wrath, despite the fact that the enclosure usurped part of his ground, but his heart pounded so much, that it was extremely difficult for him to retain his outward calm.

In this manner he spent the day. Night arrived . . . oh, if I were a painter, how wonderfully would I have depicted all the charm of the night. I would show how the whole of Mirgorod lies asleep; how immovably innumerable stars look down; how near and far the barking of the dogs resounds in the visible quietude. How past them the infatuated sexton races and climbs the wattle hedge with chivalrous intrepidity. How the white walls of the houses, embraced by moonlight, become whiter, the shadowing trees darker, their shadows blacker, the flowers and the hushed grass more fragrant, and the crickets, turbulent knights of the night, simultaneously from all sides, raise reverberating songs. I would show how in one of the low clay houses, on a lonely bed, a blackbrowed townsgirl with young trembling breasts, tosses and dreams of a hussar's moustache and spurs, while the moonlight laughs on her cheeks. I would show, how on the white road flutters the black shadow of a bat, which alights on the white chimneys of the houses . . .

But I could hardly have painted Ivan Ivanovitch, who appeared on that night with a saw in his hands. So many diverse feelings were written on his face! Quietly—quietly and stealthily he crept to the enclosure. Ivan Nikiforovitch's dogs as yet knew nothing about their quarrel and therefore allowed him, as an old friend, to approach the enclosure, the whole of which was supported by four oak posts. Having crept up to the nearest post, he placed his saw on it and began to saw. The noise caused by his work forced him to turn around every minute, but the thought of the insult restored his valor. The first post was sawn through and Ivan Ivanovitch set to work on another. His eyes burned and his fear prevented him from seeing anything. Suddenly Ivan Ivanovitch screamed and became rigid. He thought he saw a corpse, but he soon recovered, perceiving that it was a gander which had stretched out its neck towards him. Ivan Ivanovitch spat with indignation and resumed his work. The second post was sawn through as well, and the building swayed. Ivan Ivanovitch's heart pounded so terribly when he began to saw the third, that he had to interrupt his work several times. More than half of the post was sawn through, when suddenly the unsteady building tottered . . .

Ivan Ivanovitch hardly had time to jump away, when the structure collapsed with a crash. Seizing the saw he ran home in a terrible fright and threw himself on the bed, lacking even sufficient courage to look through the window at the result of his terrible deed. It seemed to him that Ivan Nikiforovitch's whole yard was teeming with people, that there was the old woman, Ivan Nikiforovitch, the boy in the endless jacket, all with clubs, and that, led by Agafya Fedosyevna, they were coming to ruin and destroy his house.

The whole of the next day Ivan Ivanovitch spent as if shaken by fever. He imagined that his hateful neighbor, in revenge for this, would, at least, set his house on fire, and so he ordered Gapka to search everywhere every minute to ascertain whether any dry straw had been placed with malignant intent. Finally, in order to forestall Ivan Nikiforovitch, he decided to issue a writ against him in the district court of Mirgorod. What it consisted of, can be learned from the next chapter.

4

*Reports what happened at a sitting of Mirgorod's district court.*

Mirgorod is a wonderful town! What buildings will you not find there! Buildings with straw roofs, with reed roofs and even with wooden roofs. There is a street to the right, there is a street to the left. A wonderful wattle hedge everywhere. Along it climb hops, on it hang pots, from behind it the sunflower shows its sunlike head, the poppy blushes, the fat marrows twinkle . . . Magnificent! The wattle hedge is always adorned with objects which make it even more colorful. There is either a petticoat on it, or a shirt or a pair of trousers. There is no thieving in Mirgorod, no pilfering, and so everybody hangs on the hedge whatever comes into his head. If you approach the town from the square, then, to be sure, you will stop for some time to admire its view. On the square is to be found a puddle, an amazing puddle! A unique puddle! Such as you have never dreamed of seeing before! It takes up almost the whole of the square. A wonderful puddle! Large and small houses, which from the distance could be taken for hayricks, gather around it and admire its beauty.

But in my opinion there is no better house than that occupied by the district court. Whether it is made of oak or birch—that is none of my business—but it has, dear sirs, eight windows! Eight windows in a row look straight into the square and into that space of water, about which I have already spoken and which the Provost calls a lake! It is the only one to be painted the color of granite. All the other houses in Mirgorod are merely white. Its roof is all of timber and would have been painted red, if the butter prepared for that purpose had not been seasoned with onions by the court clerks and eaten by them during fast days, as if to ensure that the roof should remain unpainted. A porch juts out into the square. On this hens often strut, for it is usually littered with grain or other food, not deliberately by the way, but mainly through the carelessness of litigants. The house is divided into two parts: one constitutes the court and the other contains the guard room. The part containing the court consists of two rooms. They are clean, distempered white. The front room is intended for the petitioners. In the other there is a table adorned with inkstains. On the table there is a mirror of justice and round it stand four oak chairs with high backs. Near the walls stand boxes encased in iron in which are kept stacks of local slanders. On one of these boxes stands a waxed and polished boot.

The sitting commenced early in the morning. The judge, a rather corpulent man, although somewhat slimmer than Ivan Nikiforovitch, with a kindly expression on his face, in a greasy dressing gown, with a pipe and a cup of tea, talked to the prisoner at the bar. The judge's lips were placed immediately under his nose, and so his nose could smell his upper lip to its heart's content. This lip served him instead of a snuff box, because the tobacco directed to the nose, almost always scattered over it. And thus the judge talked to the prisoner at the bar. A barefooted country girl stood on one side holding a tray with cups. At the end of the table the secretary read out the decision of the court, but in such a monotonous and mournful voice, that the prisoner himself would have fallen asleep listening to it. The judge, no doubt, would have done so before anybody else, if in the meantime an interesting conversation had not arisen.

"I purposely tried to find out," the judge was saying, sipping his tea which had already gone cold, "what they do to make them sing well. I had a nice blackbird about two years ago. And then, suddenly, it became absolutely spoiled and began to sing—Heaven knows what! The longer it went on, the worse and worse it became. It began to drawl, to croak—the least you could do was to throw it out. And it sang absolute nonsense! For the following reason: under the little neck develops a swelling, smaller than a pea. All one has to do, is to pierce this tiny swelling with a needle. Zachar Prokofyevitch taught me this. As a matter of fact, if you want to hear about it, I'll tell you how it happened. I arrive at his place . . ."

"Would you, Demyan Demyanovitch, like me to read another?" interrupted the secretary, who had already finished reading several minutes ago.

---

"And have you read it out already? Imagine, how quickly! I couldn't hear anything! And where is it? Give it to me, I'll sign it. What else have you there?"

"Cossack Bokitko's case, about the stolen cow."

"All right, read! Yes, so I arrive at his place . . . I can even tell you in detail what he regaled me with. Excellent dried sturgeon was served with the vodka. Yes, not like ours" (the judge clicked his tongue and smiled, and his nose smelled its perpetual snuff-box) . . . "to which our grocery shop treats us. I didn't take any herring, because, as you know, I often get heartburn from it. But I sampled the caviare—wonderful caviare—I should say it was superb! Then I drank some peach-brandy distilled with horse-knop. There was also some saffron-vodka, but, as you know, I don't take saffron vodka. You see, it's very good at first, as they say, to whet one's appetite, but afterwards it'll finish you . . . Ah! That's a wonderful surprise! . . ." suddenly exclaimed the judge, seeing Ivan Ivanovitch enter.

"God be with you! Good morning to you!" said Ivan Ivanovitch, bowing in all directions with his characteristic charm. My God! how he could bewitch everybody with his manners! I have never seen such refinement. He knew his own value very well and therefore considered as his due the universal respect that was paid to him.

The judge offered Ivan Ivanovitch a chair and his nose drew all the tobacco from his upper lip, which was always a sign of great satisfaction.

"What can I offer you, Ivan Ivanovitch?" he asked, "would you like a cup of tea?"

"No, thank you very much indeed," answered Ivan Ivanovitch and he bowed and sat down.

"Do me the favor, just one cup," repeated the judge.

"No, thank you. I appreciate your hospitality very much," an-

---

swered Ivan Ivanovitch and he bowed and sat down.

"One cup," repeated the judge.

"No, don't trouble, Demyan Demyanovitch." At this Ivan Ivanovitch bowed and sat down.

"A small cup."

"So be it, I might have a small cup," said Ivan Ivanovitch, and stretched out his hand to the tray.

My God! What infinite refinement some men possess! It is difficult to describe what a pleasant impression such behavior makes!

"Won't you have another small cup?"

"I thank you sincerely," answered Ivan Ivanovitch, putting the cup upside down on the tray and bowing.

"Do me the favor, Ivan Ivanovitch!"

"I can't, I'm very much obliged." At this Ivan Ivanovitch bowed and sat down.

"Ivan Ivanovitch! For friendship's sake, one small cup!"

"No, I'm extremely obliged for the treat," having said this Ivan Ivanovitch bowed and sat down.

"Only one cup! A small cup!" Ivan Ivanovitch stretched out his hand to the tray and took a cup.

The deuce! How the man can, how the man succeeds in keeping up his dignity!

"Demyan Demyanovitch, I . . ." said Ivan Ivanovitch, swallowing the last gulp of tea, "I've come to you on urgent business. I'm issuing a summons." At this Ivan Ivanovitch put down the cup and took out from his pocket a closely written sheet of stamped paper, "a summons against my enemy, a sworn enemy of mine."

"Who would that be?"

"Ivan Nikiforovitch Dovgotchkhoon."

When the judge heard these words he almost fell from the chair.

------

"What are you saying?" he said in amazement, "Ivan Ivanovitch, is it you?"

"As you see, it is I."

"God be with you and all the Saints! How can it be! You, Ivan Ivanovitch, have become Ivan Nikiforovitch's enemy! Are your lips saying it? Say it again! Isn't there somebody hidden behind you and saying it instead of you?"

"What is there incredible about it? I can't look at him. He has given me mortal offense. He has hurt my dignity."

"Holy Trinity! How can I now make my mother believe it? And every day, as soon as my sister and I quarrel, the old thing says: 'My children, you live like cat and dog with each other. If only you took Ivan Ivanovitch's and Ivan Nikiforovitch's example: what friends they are, real friends! They are pals! They are worthy people!' There you are—friends! Tell me what's all this? How did it happen?"

"This is a delicate business, Demyan Demyanovitch! You can't tell it in words, you'd better order the petition to be read. Here, take it from this side, it's more polite."

"Read it, Taras Tichonovitch!" said the judge addressing the secretary.

Taras Tichonovitch took the petition, and having cleaned his nose in the manner in which all secretaries clean their noses in district courts—by means of his two fingers—began to read:

"From the nobleman and landowner of the Mirgorod district, Ivan, son of Ivan, Pererepenko, a petition, the particulars whereof are as follows:—

"I. Notorious to the whole world for his sacrilegious disgraceful actions, the nobleman Ivan, son of Nikifor, Dovgotchkhoon, the measure of whose iniquities is full, did in this year 1810, on the 7th day of July, put a deadly affront on my personal honor, tending equally to the destruction and to the defilement of my rank and family. The same nobleman, who is in addition of base appearance, possesses a cantankerous character and abounds in blasphemies of all kinds and swear words . . ."

Here the reader stopped for a while to clean his nose again, and the judge folded his hands with reverence and said to himself: "What a vivacious pen! God Almighty! How this man writes!"

Ivan Ivanovitch asked that the reading should proceed and Taras Tichonovitch continued:

"The same nobleman Ivan, son of Nikifor, Dovgotchkhoon, when I came to him with friendly suggestions called me publicly by a name, which insults and slanders my reputation, namely, 'a gander.' Whereas as is well known to the whole of the district of Mirgorod, I have never called myself by this base animal's name and have no intention of calling myself so in the future. AND whereas in proof of my noble origin there is the following that is to say that in the register of births in the church of the Three Saints, there is entered the day of my birth as well as the baptismal name received by me. AND whereas 'a gander' as is known to everybody in the least conversant with science cannot be entered in the register of births, for 'a gander' is not a human being, but a bird, as is well known to every one even to a person who has never attended a seminary. Nevertheless the above-mentioned malignant nobleman, being conversant with all this, for no other purpose, but that of putting a deadly affront upon my rank and calling, abused me with the above mentioned base word.

"II. The above mentioned indecorous and indecent nobleman has in addition trespassed on my patrimonial estate inherited by me from my parent, blessed be his memory, Ivan, son of Onisy, Pererepenko, who appertained to the priestly calling since, contrary to all laws, he transported an enclosure of geese exactly opposite my porch, which was done with no other intention than that of intensifying the insult put upon me as up to that time the above mentioned enclosure stood in an appropriate place and was comparatively stable. But the repulsive action of the above mentioned nobleman was designed solely for the purpose of making me a witness of indecent and vulgar acts, for it is known that not every man will go on respectable business to an enclosure, especially one containing geese. During these said unlawful actions, two supporting posts were erected on ground received by me from my parent, blessed be his memory, Ivan, son of Onisy, Pererepenko, during his lifetime, which land begins from the granary and extends in a straight line to that place where the women wash pots.

"III. The above described nobleman, whose very name and surname instil the greatest repugnance of every kind, harbors in his heart an evil intention of setting me on fire in my own house. The indubitable proof of which is clear from the below-mentioned facts.

"1stly, the same malignant nobleman has begun to leave his chambers frequently, which he never undertook before, because of his laziness and the odious fatness of his body.

"2ndly, in the servant's room, which adjoins the same fence, which guards my own ground inherited by me from my deceased parent, blessed be his memory, Ivan, son of Onisy, Pererepenko, daily and for unusual length of time there burns a light which is an obvious proof of this, for until now, due to his vile avarice, not only the tallow-candle but even the lamp has always been extinguished.

"AND I therefore ask that the said nobleman, Ivan, son of Nikifor, Dovgotchkhoon, who is guilty of arson, of insulting my rank, name and surname and of rapacious annexation of my property and, most important of all, of base and wilful addition to my surname of the epithet 'gander' should be ordered to pay a fine, to pay costs and damages, and that the same, as a transgressor, be put into shackles, and having been chained be removed to the city prison, and that judgment on this my petition be given immediately and promptly. Written and composed by the nobleman and landowner of Mirgorod, Ivan, son of Ivan, Pererepenko."

After the reading of the petition, the judge came nearer to Ivan

Ivanovitch, seized him by a button and began to talk to him practically in this vein: "What are you doing, Ivan Ivanovitch? Have some fear of God! Throw the petition away, let it perish! May it dream of Satan! You'd better take Ivan Nikiforovitch by the hands and kiss each other. And buy some wine or just make some punch and invite me! We'll have a drink together and forget everything!"

"No, Demyan Demyanovitch! This matter is different," said Ivan Ivanovitch, with the dignity which always suited him so well. "This is different from an action which could be decided by a friendly agreement. Good-bye. Good-bye to you, too, gentlemen!" he continued with the same dignity, addressing everybody. "I hope that my petition will have the appropriate effect."

And he departed, leaving all the court in amazement.

The judge sat without saying a word. The secretary snuffed his tobacco. The clerks dropped the fragment of a bottle, used instead of an inkstand, and the judge himself absent-mindedly spread the ink puddle on the table with his finger.

"What do you say to this, Dorofey Trofimovitch?" said the judge after a prolonged silence, addressing the accused.

"I won't say anything," answered the accused.

"Strange things happen nowadays!" continued the judge.

Hardly had he the time to say this, when the door squeaked and the front half of Ivan Nikiforovitch appeared before the court. The remaining half was still in the hall. Ivan Nikiforovitch's appearance, especially in court, seemed so uncanny that the judge screamed, the secretary interrupted his reading, one clerk, in a semblance of a baize semi-dress coat, put his pen in his mouth. The other swallowed a fly. Even the invalid, who performed the duties of courier and guard, and who, until then, had been standing near the door scratching inside his dirty shirt, which had a badge on its sleeve, even that invalid's mouth gaped and he stepped on somebody's foot.

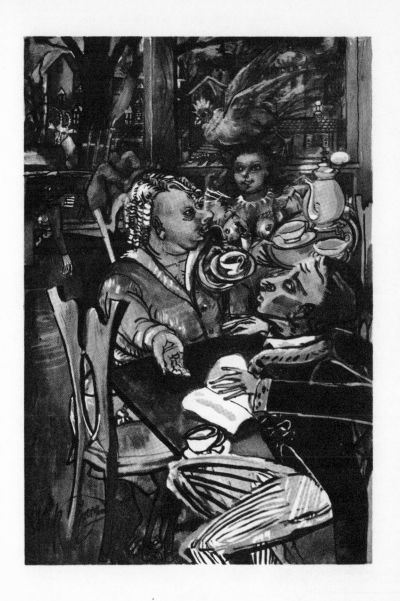

*The sitting commenced early in the morning*

"What a surprise! What brought you here and how? How is your health, Ivan Nikiforovitch?"

But Ivan Nikiforovitch was semi-conscious, for he had become wedged in the door and could not make a step either forward or backward. In vain did the judge cry out into the hall for someone there to push Ivan Nikiforovitch out into the courtroom from the back. Only one old woman petitioner was in the hall and she, despite all the efforts of her old bony hands, could not do anything. Then one of the clerks, with fat lips, wide shoulders, a thick nose, with eyes that squinted slightly and looked drunken, and with torn elbows to his jacket, approached Ivan Nikiforovitch's front half and folded both his hands across like a child's. Then he winked at the old invalid, who pushed his knee into Ivan Nikiforovitch's stomach, and despite the latter's piteous groans, he was squeezed back into the hall. Then the bolts were pushed aside and the second half of the door opened. The clerk and his assistant, the invalid, spread such a strong smell with their breath during their harmonious collaboration, that the court room transformed itself for a time into a tavern.

"They haven't hurt you, Ivan Nikiforovitch, have they? I'll tell my dear mother about it, she'll send you some lotion. If you only rub it into your waist and back, everything will be well."

But Ivan Nikiforovitch flopped heavily into a chair, and, except for prolonged groans, could say nothing. Finally, in a voice weak with exhaustion and hardly audible, he gasped, "Won't you?" and taking the pouch from his pocket added, "Have some, help yourself!"

"I'm extremely glad to see you," answered the judge, "but I still can't imagine what forced you to undergo such a strain and oblige us with such a pleasant surprise."

"A petition . . ." Ivan Nikiforovitch could only murmur.

---

"A petition? What petition?"

"A summons . . ." (Here breathlessness caused a long pause.) "Och! A summons against a scoundrel . . . Ivan, Ivan's son, Pererepenko."

"Heavens! You too! Such exceptional friends! Summons against such a worthy man . . . !"

"He is—Satan himself!" said Ivan Nikiforovitch abruptly.

The judge crossed himself.

"Take the petition, read it."

"Can't be helped, read it out, Taras Tikhonovitch," said the judge, addressing his secretary with a displeased air, while his nose involuntarily snuffed his upper lip, which he usually did only when experiencing great satisfaction. This wilfulness of his nose made the judge even more annoyed. He took out a handkerchief and swept all the tobacco from his upper lip, to punish it for its insolence.

The secretary, after the usual preliminaries performed by him before he began reading, i.e., the cleaning of his nose without the aid of a handkerchief, began to read in his usual voice, as follows:—

"Petition by a nobleman of the Mirgorod district, Ivan, son of Nikifor, Dovgotchkhoon, particulars whereof are as follows:—

"I. Because of his odious anger and obvious malevolence, Ivan, son of Ivan, Pererepenko, who calls himself a nobleman, inflicted upon me various iniquities and damages and committed other malicious and horrifying deeds in respect of me, and yesterday, like a robber and a thief, with axes, saws, chisels and other such instruments, stole into my yard at night and into my enclosure which is situate therein and with his own hands wilfully hacked it to pieces for which unlawful and rapacious deed, I, for my part, did not give him any provocation.

"II. The same nobleman, Pererepenko, harbors homicidal intentions against me and he kept these intentions secret until the 7th day of last month when he came to me and began to entreat me in a friendly and, at the same time, sly manner, to give him a

gun, which was in my room and offered me for it (with the mean-
ness characteristic of him) various paltry things such as a tawny
pig and two measures of oats. But, guessing in advance his criminal intent, I tried by various means to deflect him, but the same
crook and scoundrel, Ivan, Ivan's son, Pererepenko, swore at me
like a peasant and since that time has nurtured implacable enmity towards me. Moreover, the same frequently mentioned mad
nobleman and robber, Ivan, Ivan's son, Pererepenko, is of very
base origin: his sister was known to the whole world as a hussy
and followed a company of chasseurs which was stationed in Mirgorod about five years ago and she enrolled her husband into the
peasant's class, while his father and mother were also extremely
lawless people and were both incredible drunkards. Nevertheless,
the above-mentioned nobleman and robber, Pererepenko, with
his animal-like and immoral deeds has surpassed all his relations
and under the guise of virtue commits the most atrocious crimes:
he never observes fasts, for on the eve of Lent this atheist bought
a sheep and the next day ordered his peasant woman paramour
Gapka to slaughter it, making the excuse that he needed fat for
lamps and candles.

"Therefore I ask that the same nobleman as a robber, sacrile-
gist, scoundrel, clearly guilty of theft and robbery, be put in fet-
ters and removed to prison or the district jail and there, if it be
so decreed by the court, be soundly thrashed and, if necessary,
sent to hard labor in Siberia, and further, that he be ordered to
pay costs and damages and that a decision be made accordingly
on this my petition.

"This petition is signed and delivered by the nobleman of the
Mirgorod district, Ivan, Nikifor's son, Dovgotchkhoon."

As soon as the secretary finished reading, Ivan Nikiforovitch took
his cap and bowed with the intention of leaving.

"Where are you off to, Ivan Nikiforovitch?" the judge called out
to the departing Ivan Nikiforovitch, "Stay for a while! Have some
tea! Orishko, what are you standing about for, you silly girl, and
why are you winking at the clerks? Be off, and bring some tea!"

But Ivan Nikiforovitch, alarmed at being so far from home and at having passed through such a dangerous ordeal, had already managed to squeeze himself through the door, saying, "Don't worry, I will with pleasure . . ." and closed it behind him, leaving the whole court in amazement.

There was nothing to be done about it. Both petitions were accepted and the action was on the verge of assuming a very interesting aspect, when an unfortunate occurrence added an even greater sensation. After the judge had left the court with the accused and the secretary in attendance, and while the clerks were stuffing into a sack the hens, the eggs, the loaves of brown and white bread and

the pastry and other rubbish brought by petitioners, a brown pig rushed into the room and, to the amazement of the spectators, grabbed not the pastry nor a bread crust, but Ivan Nikiforovitch's petition, which lay on the end of the table with its sheets hanging down. Having seized the papers, the brown pig ran away so quickly that despite the rulers and inkstands which were hurled, not one of the clerks could catch up with it.

This extraordinary occurrence caused a tremendous upheaval, because the petition had not even been copied. The judge, or rather his secretary, and the accused discussed for a long time this unprecedented occurrence. Finally, it was decided to write out a report to the Provost, as investigation of this matter appertained to the department of the town police. The report headed No. 389 was sent to him that very day. There was a very peculiar sequel, the nature of which the readers may learn from the following chapter.

## 5

*In which is described the conference between two persons respected in Mirgorod.*

As soon as Ivan Ivanovitch had dealt with his household affairs and had left as usual to rest under the awning, he saw, to his extreme amazement, something red twinkle at his gate. It was the red lapel of the Provost who, like his collar, had received a varnishing and at the edges had lacquered skin.

Ivan Ivanovitch thought to himself, "It's not bad, that Peter Fedorovitch has come to have a chat," but became very surprised when he saw that the Provost walked extremely quickly and waved his hands, a thing he did very seldom.

Eight buttons were placed on the Provost's uniform. The ninth, which tore itself away during a procession to consecrate a church two years ago, has still not been found by the police, although the Provost, when accepting the daily reports made to him by the police inspectors, always asks whether the button has yet been found. These eight buttons were planted on him in the manner in which the peasant women plant beans: one to the right, another to the left. His left foot had been shot through during the last campaign, and in consequence, limping, he thrust this foot so far to the side that he almost frustrated the efforts of his right foot. The quicker the Provost manoeuvred his infantry, the slower he moved forward, and so, before he reached the awning, Ivan Ivanovitch had enough time to puzzle over the reason which made the Provost wave his hands so quickly. It was all the more intriguing, as the business appeared to be of unusual importance, since the Provost wore even his new sabre.

"Good morning, Peter Fedorovitch!" exclaimed Ivan Ivanovitch, who, as had been mentioned before, was extremely curious and could not restrain his impatience at the sight of the Provost, who stormed the porch without raising his eyes and quarrelled with his infantry, which on no account could climb up the step at one go.

"Good day to my dear friend and benefactor, Ivan Ivanovitch," answered the Provost.

"Do me the favor to sit down. I see you're tired, because your wounded foot is in the way . . ."

"My foot!" exclaimed the Provost, throwing at Ivan Ivanovitch one of those glances which a giant casts at a pygmy, a learned pedant at a dancing master. At this he stretched out his leg and stamped it on the floor. This audacity, however, cost him dear, for his whole body swayed and his nose pecked at the banisters. The wise guardian of law and order, to hide this, immediately straightened himself out and put his hand into his pocket as if intending to get out his snuffbox.

"Let me tell you, my dear friend and benefactor, Ivan Ivanovitch, that in my time I've taken part in more difficult campaigns than this. Yes, I certainly have. For example, during the campaign of 1807. Ach, let me tell you how I climbed over a fence after a pretty German girl." At this the Provost closed one eye and a devilishly roguish smile spread over his lips.

"Where have you been to-day?" asked Ivan Ivanovitch, wishing to interrupt the Provost and to lead him more quickly to the reason for his visit. He wanted very much to ask the Provost point-blank about the object of this visit, but his expert knowledge of the ways of society confronted him with all the indecency of such a direct question and Ivan Ivanovitch, his heart beating with unusual vigor, had to contain himself and await the solution of the puzzle.

"With your permission, I'll tell you where I've been," answered the Provost. "Firstly, may I say, the weather is excellent to-day . . ."

Ivan Ivanovitch almost died on hearing the last words.

"With your permission," continued the Provost, "I have come to you to-day on important business."

The Provost's face and demeanor assumed the same preoccupied air with which he had stormed the porch.

Ivan Ivanovitch's spirits revived and he trembled as if shaken by fever. Without any delay, as was his wont, he put the question:

"What's important about it? Is it really important?"

"Well, you will see. First of all, let me tell you, dear friend and benefactor, Ivan Ivanovitch, that you . . . as far as I am concerned, please appreciate, I've nothing to do with it, it's the Government's requirement that makes it necessary. You've disturbed the good order of the parish."

---

"What are you saying, Peter Feodorovitch? I can't understand a word."

"Have a heart, Ivan Ivanovitch. Why can't you understand? Your own animal has stolen a very important Government paper and you can still maintain, after all this, that you don't understand anything?"

"What animal?"

"If I may say so, your brown pig."

"What has it got to do with me? Why does the court caretaker keep the doors open?"

"But, Ivan Ivanovitch, your own animal, that means that you're guilty!"

"I'm obliged to you for comparing me with a pig."

"But I didn't say that at all, Ivan Ivanovitch. By God, I didn't. Be kind, let your conscience be the judge. It's known to you, no doubt, that according to the decision of the authorities, it's prohibited for unclean animals to stroll about town, especially in the main street. You'll admit yourself, that this is prohibited."

"God knows what you're talking about. What if a pig did get out into the street!"

"Allow me to inform you, allow me, allow me, Ivan Ivanovitch, that that's quite impossible. What can be done? The authorities decide—we have to obey. I don't dispute that hens sometimes run into the street and even into the square and also geese. But please note: hens and geese. Only last year I ordered pigs and goats not to be let out into the squares, and I ordered that instruction to be read aloud, word for word, in assembly, before the whole of the people."

"No, Peter Feodorovitch, I can't understand anything except your attempts to offend me in every way."

"You can't say, dearest friend and benefactor, that I'm trying to offend you. Remember: I didn't say a word to you last year, when you built a roof more than two feet higher than the established height. On the contrary, I pretended not to notice it at all. Believe me, dearest friend, that now too I would absolutely, so to say . . . but my duty, in short, obligation demands that I ensure cleanliness. Judge for yourself, what, when suddenly in the main street . . ."

"And how good your main streets are! Every peasant woman goes there to throw out everything she doesn't need."

"May I inform you, Ivan Ivanovitch, that it's you who are offending me! It's true that it sometimes happens, but in the main only under the fences, the barns and the granaries, but for a sow with its young to barge into the main street, into the square, that is a grave matter . . ."

"What is this, Peter Feodorovitch! A pig, after all, is God's creation!"

"I agree. It's known to the whole world, that you're a learned man, who cultivates all sciences and various other subjects. Of course, I never cultivated any sciences. I began to learn shorthand in the thirtieth year of my life. After all, as you'll know, I'm from the common people."

"Ahem," said Ivan Ivanovitch.

"Yes," continued the Provost, "in the year 1801 I was a lieutenant in the 42 Chasseur Regiment, 4th Company. Our regimental commander, if you wish to know, was Captain Yeremeyev."

At this the Provost dived with his fingers into the snuffbox which Ivan Ivanovitch held open and kneaded the tobacco.

Ivan Ivanovitch answered: "Ahem."

"But my duty," continued the Provost, "is to obey the orders of the Government. Do you know, Ivan Ivanovitch, that one who steals Government papers from courts is liable, as for other crimes, to trial at the criminal court?"

"I know it so well, that if you wish, I could teach you something about it too. Namely: it applies to all human beings. It would apply to you, for example, had you stolen some papers. But a pig is an animal, God's creation."

"That is so, but the law says Guilty of robbery . . . I would ask you to listen more attentively! Guilty! Here, neither kind, sex, nor rank is denoted, which means an animal can be guilty as well. It is as you wish, but the animal has to be produced in court as a disturber of peace, for its punishment to be decided.

"No, Peter Feodorovitch," coolly contradicted Ivan Ivanovitch. "That shall not be."

"As you wish, but I have to follow the Government's instructions."

"Are you trying to intimidate me? You probably want to send the handless soldier to fetch it? I'll order the servant woman to show him out with a poker and to break his remaining hand."

"I don't dare to quarrel with you. If you don't want to produce it to the police, use it as you desire. Slaughter it, if you wish, for Christmas and make hams from it or eat it raw. Only I'd like to ask you, if you make any sausages, send me a couple of those that Gapka makes so well from pig's blood and fat. My Agrafena Trofimovna is very fond of them."

"You're welcome. I'll send you a couple of sausages."

"I'll be extremely grateful to you, dear friend and benefactor. Now allow me to tell you only one more thing. I've been instructed by the judge as well as by all your acquaintances, so to speak, to make peace between you and your friend Ivan Nikiforovitch."

"What! With that boor! That I should make peace with that churl! Never! It'll never be, never!" Ivan Ivanovitch was in an extremely resolute state of mind.

"As you wish," answered the Provost, treating both his nostrils to some tobacco, "I don't dare to advise you. Nevertheless allow me to tell you, you are quarrelling now, but when you make peace . . ."

But Ivan Ivanovich began to talk about quail-catching, which he usually did when he wanted to change the subject.

And so the Provost had to depart home without achieving any success.

### 6

*From which the reader can easily find out everything it contains.*

Despite the efforts of the Court to hush the matter up, the very next day the whole of Mirgorod found out that Ivan Ivanovitch's pig had stolen Ivan Nikiforovitch's petition. The Provost, losing control over himself, was the first to blurt it out. When Ivan Nikiforovitch was told about it, he did not say anything and only asked: "Was it the brown one?"

But Agafya Fedosyevna, who was present at the time, began to attack Ivan Nikiforovitch again: "What are you going to do about it, Ivan Nikiforovitch? They'll laugh at you, call you a fool, if you let it go at this. What sort of a nobleman will you be after this? You'll be worse than the peasant woman, who sells the sweets you like so much."

And the turbulent woman prevailed upon him! She found somewhere a middle-aged, swarthy man, with spots all over his face, who wore a dark blue jacket patched at the elbows, who in all respects resembled an office inkstand. He greased his boots with tar, carried three quills behind his ear and had a glass phial, instead of an inkstand, tied to a button by a string. He would eat nine tarts at one sitting and would put the tenth in his pocket, and on one stamped sheet of paper wrote down such a miscellany of slander, that not a single clerk could read it at one sitting without interspersing his reading with coughing and sneezing. This miniature likeness of a man, rummaged, pondered, wrote, and, finally, concocted the following paper:—

"To the Mirgorod District Court from the Nobleman Ivan, Nikifor's son, Dovgotchkhoon, as a sequel to my petition which came from me the Nobleman Ivan, Nikifor's son, Dovgotchkhoon, and which related to the Nobleman Ivan, Ivan's son, Pererepenko, with whom the Mirgorod District Court has acted in collusion.

"WHEREAS it was sought to keep secret that the brown pig imprudently took the law in its hand, but the news has already reached the ears of the outside world, AND WHEREAS this collusion, being of evil design, should be immediately referred to the jurisdiction of the High Court since a pig is a foolish animal, all the less capable of stealing the document and it obviously follows that the before-mentioned pig must have been incited to this act by the same enemy, who calls himself the nobleman Ivan, Ivan's son, Pererepenko, who has been already detected in robbery, attempted murder and blasphemy. AND WHEREAS the Mirgorod Court with partiality characteristic of it, concluded a secret agreement, without which the pig could on no account gain entrance to steal the document, for the Mirgorod District Court is extremely well supplied with officials in proof of which one has only to name one soldier, who always stays in the outer room and who, although he squints in one eye and has a somewhat damaged hand, nevertheless is fully capable of driving out a pig and striking it with a cudgel, all which unquestionably proves connivance of the Mirgorod Court and that there was a prior agreement to divide a bribe. NOW THEREFORE I, the Nobleman Ivan, Nikifor's son, Dovgotchkhoon, hereby notify the District Court for its full information that if the said petition is not exacted from that brown pig or from the Nobleman, Pererepenko, its abettor, and if judgment is not given in my favor as is my due, then I, the Nobleman, Ivan, Nikifor's son, Dovgotchkhoon, will lodge in the High Court a complaint about such unlawful collusion by the District Court with all the necessary formalities.

"Nobleman of the Mirgorod District, Ivan, Nikifor's son, Dovgotchkhoon."

This petition had its effect. The judge was a man, as all good people usually are, of cowardly disposition. He turned to the secretary. But the secretary blew through his lips a thick "Ahem" and showed on his face that equivocal and devilishly ambiguous expression which Satan assumes when he sees his prey rush to fall at his feet. One remedy remained: to make peace between the two friends. How was it to be achieved, when all previous attempts had been so unsuccessful? Nevertheless, they decided to try. But Ivan Ivanovitch declared bluntly that he had no such desire, and even became extremely annoyed. Ivan Nikiforovitch, instead of answering, turned his back on them and did not say a single word.

After this the proceedings commenced with that amazing speed for which the law courts are famous. The document was marked, entered, numbered, sewn up, signed—everything on the same day —and then put into a cupboard, where it lay for a year, a second year, a third year. A multitude of brides had managed to get married in the meantime. A new street was cut through Mirgorod. The judge lost a double tooth and two incisors. More children ran about in Ivan Ivanovitch's yard than before (where they came from God alone knows). . . . To rebuke Ivan Ivanovitch, Ivan Nikiforovitch built a new enclosure for geese, although somewhat further away than the first one, and completely blocked himself off, so that these worthy people rarely saw each other face to face. And the document, taking the normal course, still lay in a cupboard, which had turned marble from ink stains.

In the meantime an event occurred of the greatest importance for the whole of Mirgorod. The Provost gave a party! Where can I obtain brush and paint to describe the variety of the assembly and the magnificent banquet? Take a watch, open it and look at what goes on inside! What tomfoolery, is it not? Well, now imagine almost as many, if not more, wheels standing in the middle of the Provost's yard. What a variety of britchkas and carts! One had a broad beam and a narrow front. Another—a narrow beam and a broad front. One was a combination of a britchka and a cart, another resembled neither a britchka nor a cart. One resembled a huge hay-rick or a fat merchant's wife. Another resembled a dishevelled Jew or a skeleton which had not yet freed itself from its skin. Another's profile was precisely like the stem of a pipe. Another did not resemble anything and looked a queer creature, quite hideous and extremely fantastic. From amid this chaos of wheels and coach-boxes towered a semblance of a coach fitted with an ordinary house window protected with thick window bars. The drivers, dressed in gray overcoats and jackets, with sheepskin caps and forage caps of various types, with pipes in their hands, attended to the unharnessed horses in the yard.

What a party the Provost gave! Allow me to enumerate all who were there. Taras Tarasovitch, Yevpl Akinfovitch, Yevtichy Yevtichyevitch, Ivan Ivanovitch—not our Ivan Ivanovitch, but another—Savva Gavrilovitch, our Ivan Ivanovitch, Yelefery Yeleferyevitch, Makar Nazaryevitch, Foma Grigoryevitch . . . I can't go on! The hand grows tired of writing them! And how many ladies there were! Swarthy and pale faced, long and short, fat, like Ivan Nikiforovitch, and some so thin that it seemed each of them could be hidden in the Provost's sword sheath. How many women's caps! How many dresses! Red, yellow, coffee-colored, green, blue, new, turned, recut—scarves, ribbons, handbags! Good-bye, poor eyes! You will be good for nothing after this spectacle. And what a long table was stretched out! And how talkative everybody became. What a noise there was! In comparison what is a mill with all its grindstones, cog-wheels, driving wheels, mortars! I cannot tell you for certain what they talked about, but I should think they discussed many pleasant and useful things, such as the weather, dogs, wheat, women's caps, colts.

Finally, Ivan Ivanovitch—not our Ivan Ivanovitch, but another —whose one eye squints, said: "It seems very strange to me that my right eye" (the squinting Ivan Ivanovitch always referred to himself ironically) "doesn't see Ivan Nikiforovitch Dovgotchkhoon, Esq."

"He didn't want to come," said the Provost.

"Why is that?"

"God be praised, two years have passed now since they quarrelled, that is Ivan Ivanovitch with Ivan Nikiforovitch, and where one is, the other will on no account go."

"What are you saying?" As he spoke the squinting Ivan Ivanovitch raised his eyes to Heaven and folded his hands together: "If people with good eyes do not live in peace, how can I live peacefully with my squinting eye?"

Everybody laughed loudly at these words. Everybody was very fond of the squinting Ivan Ivanovitch, for he made jokes entirely in accordance with modern taste. Even the tall, thinnish man in a baize jacket with a plaster on his nose, who until then had sat in a corner and had not once changed the expression on his face, not even when a fly flew into his nose—that same gentleman rose from his seat and moved nearer to the crowd which surrounded the squinting Ivan Ivanovitch.

"Listen," said the squinting Ivan Ivanovitch, when he saw that a considerable crowd had encircled him: "Listen! Instead of peeping into my squinting eye, let's reconcile our two friends! Now that Ivan Ivanovitch is chatting to the women and girls—let's quietly send for Ivan Nikiforovitch and then let us push them together."

Ivan Ivanovitch's suggestion was unanimously accepted and it was decided immediately to send for Ivan Nikiforovitch, and to persuade him, at any cost, to drive to the Provost's dinner. But the important question: whom to entrust with this vital mission, perplexed everybody. They argued for a long time as to who was the most capable and skilled in diplomatic errands. Finally it was unanimously decided to entrust Anton Prokofyevitch Golopuzy with the whole task.

But it is necessary first to tell the reader something about this remarkable person. Anton Prokofyevitch was an absolutely virtuous man, in the full sense of the word. If any of the notables of Mirgorod gives him a scarf or some underwear—he expresses his thanks. If anyone raps his nose slightly—he will express his thanks too. When he was asked, "Why, Anton Prokofyevitch, is it that your jacket is brown, but its sleeves light blue?" he would always reply, "And haven't you got one like that? You wait. It'll wear down and it will all become the same color!" And indeed, the light blue cloth began to turn brown from the effect of the sun and now it completely matches the color of the jacket. But the strange thing is, that Anton Prokofyevitch is in the habit of wearing woolen clothes in the summer, and nankeen clothes in the winter. Anton Prokofyevitch does not possess a house of his own. He had one formerly at the end of the town, but he sold it and with the proceeds of the sale bought three bay horses and a smallish britchka, in which he drove to visit landowners. But as there was a lot of trouble connected with the horses and moreover money was needed for oats,

Anton Prokofyevitch exchanged them for a violin and a servant girl, and a twenty-five rouble note. Then Anton Prokofyevitch sold the violin and exchanged the girl for a morocco leather tobacco pouch embroidered with gold and now he possesses a tobacco pouch such as nobody else has. Thanks to this luxury he can no longer drive about the village and has to remain in town and spends his nights in various houses, especially in those belonging to noblemen who find pleasure in rapping his nose. Anton Prokofyevitch likes to eat well and is proficient in all kinds of drawing-room games. It was always his nature to obey, and therefore taking his cap and stick he immediately departed on his way.

As he walked he began to consider how he could induce Ivan Nikiforovitch to come to the party. The somewhat gruff character of that, by the way, worthy man made Anton Prokofyevitch's undertaking almost impossible. And then, really, how could Ivan Nikiforovitch decide to go, when even rising from bed presented great difficulty to him? And assuming that he would get up, how could he go where, as he undoubtedly knew, his implacable enemy would be? The longer Anton Prokofyevitch pondered the more obstacles he found. The day was fragrant. The sun scorched. Sweat poured from him in streams. Anton Prokofyevtich, despite being rapped on the nose, was rather a shrewd man in many ways, only he was not very lucky in bartering. He knew well when to act the fool and could sometimes disentangle himself from circumstances and situations, out of which an intelligent man can seldom extricate himself.

While his cunning mind was concocting means to persuade Ivan Nikiforovitch and he was already bravely preparing to meet any contingency, an unexpected occurrence somewhat demoralized him. At this point it would do no harm to inform the reader that one pair of Anton Prokofyevitch's pantaloons was of such a strange nature, that whenever he put them on the dogs invariably bit his legs. As ill luck would have it, on that day he had put on the very same pantaloons and so hardly had he abandoned himself to his meditations, when from all sides terrifying barks arose. Anton Prokofyevitch let out such screams (nobody could scream louder than he did) that a rush was made towards him not only by a woman he knew and the inmate of an immeasurable jacket, but even by the boys scattered about Ivan Ivanovitch's yard. Although the dogs had managed to bite only one of his legs, this considerably diminished his valor and it was a little fearfully that he advanced to the porch.

7

*and the last*

"Ah, hello! Why do you tease the dogs?" said Ivan Nikiforovitch when he saw Anton Prokofyevitch, for nobody talked to Anton Prokofyevitch except in a jocular way.

"May they all perish! Who's teasing them?" answered Anton Prokofyevitch.

"You're lying."

"By God, I'm not! Peter Feodorovitch wants you to come to dinner."

"Ahem!"

"By God, I can't tell you how insistent he was. 'Why,' he says, 'does Ivan Nikiforovitch shun me like an enemy? He never calls for a chat, or on a visit.' "

Ivan Nikiforovitch stroked his chin.

"He says 'If Ivan Nikiforovitch won't come even this time, then I know what to think. He probably has some evil intentions. Do me a favor, Anton Prokofyevitch, prevail upon him!' What about it, Ivan Nikiforovitch, shall we go? There's a fine crowd there!"

Ivan Nikiforovitch began to scrutinize a cockerel, which stood on the porch crowing with all its might.

"If you only knew, Ivan Nikiforovitch," continued the zealous deputy, "what sturgeon meat, what fresh caviare has been sent to Peter Feodorovitch."

Ivan Nikiforovitch turned his head and began to listen attentively.

This encouraged Anton Prokofyevitch: "Let's hurry. Foma Grigoryevitch is there as well! What about it?" he added, seeing that Ivan Nikiforovitch was still lying in the same position: "Are we going or aren't we?"

"Don't want to."

This "don't want to" stunned Anton Prokofyevitch. He had already thought that his persuasive description had entirely won over this, by the way, worthy man, but all he heard was a resolute "don't want to."

"Why don't you want to?" he asked almost with annoyance, an emotion he rarely displayed, not even when people put burning paper on his head, a pastime in which the judge and the Provost especially like to indulge.

Ivan Nikiforovitch snuffed some tobacco.

"As you wish, Ivan Nikiforovitch, but I don't know what's keeping you back."

"Why should I go?" said Ivan Nikiforovitch, after a long pause. "The robber will be there." It was thus he usually referred to Ivan Ivanovitch . . . God Almighty! And not long ago . . .

---

"I swear he won't be! As God is Holy, he won't! May I be struck by thunder in this very spot!" answered Anton Prokofyevitch, who was ready to swear an oath ten times in an hour. "Let's go, Ivan Nikiforovitch."

"But you're lying, Anton Prokofyevitch. He must be there."

"By God, by God, he's not! May I never move from this place if he's there! Think for yourself, what reason have I to lie? May my hands and legs wither off . . . ! What, don't you believe me even now? May I drop dead right here before you! May neither my father nor my mother, nor I myself see Heaven! Don't you still believe me?"

Ivan Nikiforovitch was completely reassured by these protestations and ordered his personal attendant, in the limitless jacket, to bring him his loose trousers and his nankeen Cossack coat.

I assume that to describe how Ivan Nikiforovitch put on his loose trousers, how a tie was wound around him, and, lastly, how they put on him the Cossack coat which burst under the left sleeve, is entirely superfluous. It will suffice to say that during the whole of that time he retained a suitable composure and did not answer a word to Anton Prokofyevitch's proposals about exchanging something for the latter's Turkish tobacco pouch.

In the meantime, the assembly awaited with impatience the decisive moment . . . when Ivan Nikiforovitch would appear and when, at last, the universal wish would be realized and these two worthy people reconciled. Many were almost sure that Ivan Nikiforovitch would not come. The Provost even offered to bet with the squinting Ivan Ivanovitch, that he would not arrive. They failed to agree only because the squinting Ivan Ivanovitch demanded that the Provost should stake his wounded leg, and he would stake his squinting eye.

# THE TWO IVANS

This hurt the Provost very much, at which the assembly laughed. Nobody had yet sat down at the table although it had long before struck two o'clock—the hour at which in Mirgorod, even on state occasions, dinner is over.

No sooner had Anton Prokofyevitch appeared in the doorway, than he was immediately surrounded. Anton Prokofyevitch shouted in reply to all questions a resolute, "He won't come!" As soon as he said this a flood of reproaches, swearing, and possibly blows was about to fall on·his head for his unsuccessful mission, when suddenly the door opened and Ivan Nikiforovitch walked in.

Had Satan himself or a corpse appeared they would not have caused such a stir as was caused by Ivan Nikiforovitch's unexpected arrival. And all Anton Prokofyevitch did was to break out into peals of laughter, holding his sides with joy at fooling the whole assembly.

Apart from anything else, everyone was astonished that Ivan Nikiforovitch should have dressed as behooves a nobleman in such a short time. Ivan Ivanovitch was not present at the time. He had gone out for some reason. Having recovered from amazement, the crowd took an interest in Ivan Nikiforovitch's health and expressed satisfaction at his spreading width. Ivan Nikiforovitch kissed everybody, saying, "Much obliged."

In the meantime, the smell of borshtch wafted across the room and tickled pleasantly the nostrils of the hungry guests. All thronged into the dining room. A file of ladies, talkative and taciturn, emaciated and fat, trooped in front, and the long table began to scintillate in all colors.

I will not describe all the dishes which were on the table. I will say nothing about either the *mnishki* [dish of flour and cream cheese] with sour cream, or the tripe *utribka,* which were served with the borshtch, or about the turkey with plums and raisins, or about that dish which, in appearance, closely resembles high boots soaked in kvass, or about the sauce which is the swan song of an ancient chef, or about the sauce served embraced by a wine flame which very much entertained and at the same time frightened the ladies. I will not begin talking about these dishes, for I very much prefer eating them to enlarging upon them in conversation.

Ivan Ivanovitch was very pleased with the fish cooked with horse-radish. He became intently engaged in the useful and nourishing exercise of disposing of it. Selecting the thinnest fish bones, he was putting them on the plate and somehow inadvertently looked across the table. Heavenly Creator! How strange it was! Opposite him sat Ivan Nikiforovitch!

At the same moment Ivan Nikiforovitch looked up, too! No! . . . I cannot . . . Give me another quill! Mine has wilted, it is dead. It is too thinly split for this picture! Their faces, with amazement mirrored in them, became as if turned to stone. Each saw a familiar face, a face each was involuntarily ready to welcome like an un-expected friend, and to offer the tobacco pouch with the words, "Help yourself," or "May I ask you to do me the honor?" but at the same time a face of horror—like an evil omen! Perspiration poured in torrents from Ivan Ivanovitch and Ivan Nikiforovitch.

All those present, all who were at the table, became numb with attention and fixed their eyes on the former friends. The ladies, who until then had been engaged in a rather interesting conversation about how capons were made, suddenly ceased their chatter. Everything became quiet. It was a picture worthy of a great painter's brush.

At last Ivan Ivanovitch took out a handkerchief and began to blow his nose, and Ivan Nikiforovitch glanced around and fixed his eyes on the open door. The Provost immediately interpreted this movement and ordered the door to be closed more firmly. Then each of the friends began to eat and not once did they look at each other again.

As soon as dinner was finished both former friends jumped up from their seats and began to look for their caps in order to slip off. Then the Provost winked, and Ivan Ivanovitch—not our Ivan Ivanovitch, but the other, the one with the squinting eye—placed himself behind Ivan Nikiforovitch and the Provost went behind Ivan Ivanovitch's back, and both began to push from behind in order to force them together and not to release them until they shook hands. Ivan Ivanovitch—the one with the squinting eye—pushed Ivan Nikiforovitch, somewhat askew, but, nevertheless, quite successfully up to where Ivan Ivanovitch stood. But the Provost set a course too much to one side. For he was quite unable to control his own obstinate infantry, which on this occasion paid no heed to any command and, as if on purpose, stepped on so vigorously in the opposite direction (which may possibly have been due to the varied assortment of liqueurs on the table) that Ivan Ivanovitch was thrown on a lady in a red dress, who in her curiosity had pushed herself out into the very middle of the room. This seemed to be a bad omen. Nevertheless, the judge, in order to improve matters, took over the Provost's place and, drawing into his nose all the tobacco from his upper lip, pushed Ivan Ivanovitch in the other direction. This is the usual method of reconciliation in Mirgorod. It somewhat resembles a game of ball. As soon as the judge had pushed Ivan Ivanovitch, Ivan Ivanovitch with the squinting eye, heaving with all his strength, pushed Ivan Nikiforovitch, from whom perspiration poured like rainwater from a roof. Despite the fact that both friends resisted extremely strongly, they were finally pushed together, because both teams received considerable reinforcements from the other guests.

Immediately they were closely surrounded on all sides and were not released until they decided to shake hands with each other.

"God preserve you, Ivan Nikiforovitch and Ivan Ivanovitch! Admit frankly: why did you quarrel? Wasn't it over some trifle? Aren't you ashamed before people and God?"

"I don't know," said Ivan Nikiforovitch, puffing with weariness (it was noticeable that he was not at all disinclined to be reconciled). "I don't know what I've done to Ivan Ivanovitch or why he sawed down my enclosure and planned to destroy me."

"I'm not guilty of any evil intent," said Ivan Ivanovitch without directing his eyes at Ivan Nikiforovitch. "I swear before God and before you, honorable nobility, that I have done nothing to my enemy. Why, then, does he insult me and slander my rank and calling?"

"What harm have I done to you, Ivan Ivanovitch?" said Ivan Nikiforovitch.

One more minute of explanation—and the old feud would be ready to die. Ivan Nikiforovitch was already putting his hand in his pocket to get out his pouch and say, "Help yourself."

"Isn't it harmful," answered Ivan Ivanovitch, without raising his eyes, "dear sir, to have insulted my rank and family with a word, which it is indecent to mention in this place?"

"Allow me to tell you as a friend, Ivan Ivanovitch" (at this Ivan Nikiforovitch touched with his finger Ivan Ivanovitch's button, which signified his complete benevolence), "that you took exception, the Devil knows why, because I called you a gander . . ."

Ivan Nikiforovitch suddenly perceived that by uttering this word he had committed an indiscretion. But it was too late, the word was

said. Everything went to the Devil! If Ivan Ivanovitch lost control of himself and became so furious—so furious that may God prevent you from seeing a man in such a rage—at the utterance of that word without witnesses, judge for yourselves, dear readers, what was the effect now, when that deadly word was pronounced in an assembly which included a multitude of ladies before whom Ivan Ivanovitch liked to be especially proper? Had Ivan Nikiforovitch not acted in such a manner, had he said "a bird," and not "a gander," it could have been remedied. But—everything was finished!

Ivan Ivanovitch cast a glance at Ivan Nikiforovitch—and what a glance! If this glance had been given executive power, it would have turned Ivan Nikiforovitch to dust. The guests understood that glance and hurried to separate them. And that man, an example of amiability, who did not let a single beggar-woman pass by without questioning her, ran out in a terrible rage. These strong storms bring out passions.

For a whole month nothing was heard of Ivan Ivanovitch. He locked himself up in his house. The inviolable trunk was opened. From the trunk were taken out—what? Silver roubles! Grandfather's old silver roubles! These silver roubles passed over into the stained hands of inky hedge-lawyers. The case was transferred to the High Court. And only when Ivan Ivanovitch received the glad news that the next day the action would be heard in court, did he come out into the light and decided to leave the house. Alas! From that time on, he was informed daily for the next ten years that the case would be finished the next day.

About five years ago I passed through the town of Mirgorod. I travelled at a bad time. It was in the autumn, with its sadly damp weather, mud and fog. Some unnatural herbage—creation of tedious uninterrupted rains—covered with sparse net the meadows and the cornfields, which it suited as pranks befit an old man, or roses an old woman. At that time the weather influenced me greatly! I was sad, when it was sad. But despite this, when I began to approach Mirgorod I felt my heart beat faster. Heavens, how many memories! I had not seen Mirgorod for twelve years. Then there lived here in touching friendship two unique men, two unique friends. And how many famous people had passed away! The judge, Demyan Demyanovitch, was already a dead man. Ivan Ivanovitch, with the squinting eye, had also taken leave of the world. I arrived in the main street. Everywhere stood poles with bunches of straw tied at their tops: some new planning was in progress! Several houses were demolished. Remnants of fences and hedges protruded dismally.

It was a feast day. I ordered my matted tilt-cart to stop before the church and I entered so quietly that nobody turned around. It is true there was nobody to do so: the church was almost empty. There was hardly anybody there. It was obvious that even the most devout had been frightened by the mud. Candles in the dull, or shall I better say, sick day, were somehow strangely unpleasant. The dark entrances were sad. The oblong windows with rounded glass were drenched with tears of rain. I stepped back into the entrance and accosted a venerable old man with hair gone grey.

"Allow me to ask you whether Ivan Nikiforovitch is alive?"

At that moment the image lamp flickered more vividly before the ikon and the light flashed straight into my neighbor's face. How amazed was I, when I looked closer, to see familiar features! It was Ivan Nikiforovitch himself! But how changed!

"How's your health, Ivan Nikiforovitch? You have aged!"

"Yes, I have aged. I've come to-day from Poltava," answered Ivan Nikiforovitch.

"What are you saying? You travelled to Poltava in such bad weather?"

---

"What can I do? My case . . ."

At this I involuntarily sighed.

Ivan Nikiforovitch heard the sigh and said, "Don't worry, I've reliable information that the action will be decided next week, in my favor."

I shrugged my shoulders and left to find out something about Ivan Ivanovitch.

"Ivan Ivanovitch is here," somebody told me, "he's in the choir."

Then I saw an emaciated figure. Was that truly Ivan Ivanovitch? His face was covered with wrinkles, his hair was entirely white, but the fur coat was still the same. After a preliminary greeting, Ivan Ivanovitch turned to me with the cheerful smile, which always so well suited his funnel-shaped face, and said:—

"Shall I impart some pleasant news to you?"

"What news?" I asked.

"To-morrow my action will be definitely decided. The tribunal said that was certain."

I sighed even deeper and hurriedly said good-bye—for I was travelling on some very important business—and sat down in the tilt-cart.

The emaciated horses, famous in Mirgorod under the name of courier horses, began to drag along, making with their hooves, steeped in the grey mass of mud, a sound unpleasant to the ears. The rain poured in buckets on the Jew who sat on the coach-box and who had covered himself with a mat. The damp went through me. The sad town gate with the sentry box, in which there was only an invalided serviceman mending his gray armor, passed slowly by. Again the same meadows, partly ploughed, black and in parts green, wet jackdaws and ravens, monotonous rain, a tearful sky without a chink of light. The world is a melancholy place, gentlemen!

---

# THE

# OVERCOAT

I N THE department of . . . but I had better not mention in what department. There is nothing in the world more readily moved to wrath than a department, a regiment, a government office, and in fact any sort of official body. Nowadays every private individual considers all society insulted in his person. I have been told that very lately a petition was handed in from a police-captain of what town I don't recollect, and that in this petition he set forth clearly that the institutions of the State were in danger and that its sacred name was being taken in vain; and, in proof thereof, he appended to his petition an enormously long volume of some work of romance in which a police-captain appeared on every tenth page, occasionally, indeed, in an intoxicated condition. And so, to avoid any unpleasantness, we had better call the department of which we are speaking a certain department.

And so, in a certain department there was a government clerk; a clerk of whom it cannot be said that he was very remarkable; he was short, somewhat pockmarked, with rather reddish hair and rather dim, bleary eyes, with a small bald patch on the top of his head, with wrinkles on both sides of his cheeks and the sort of complexion which is usually associated with hæmorrhoids . . . no help for that, it is the Petersburg climate. As for his grade in the service (for among us the grade is what must be put first), he was what is called a perpetual titular councillor, a class at which, as we all know, various writers who indulge in the praiseworthy habit of attacking those who cannot defend themselves jeer and jibe to their hearts' content. This clerk's surname was Bashmatchkin. From the very name it is clear that it must have been derived from a shoe (*bashmak*); but when and under what circumstances it was derived from a shoe, it is impossible to say. Both his father and his grandfather and even his brother-in-law, and all the Bashmatchkins without exception wore boots, which they simply re-soled two or three times a year. His name was Akaky Akakyevitch. Perhaps it may strike the reader as a rather strange and far-fetched name, but I can assure him that it was not far-fetched at all, that the circumstances were such that it was quite out of the question to give him any other name. Akaky Akakyevitch was born towards nightfall, if my memory does not deceive me, on the twenty-third of March. His mother, the wife of a government clerk, a very good woman, made arrangements in due course to christen the child. She was still lying in bed, facing the door, while on her right hand stood the godfather, an excellent man called Ivan Ivanovitch Yeroshkin, one of the head clerks in the Senate, and the godmother, the wife of a police official, and a woman of rare qualities, Arina Semyonovna Byelobryushkov. Three names were offered to the happy mother for selection— Moky, Sossy, or the name of the martyr Hozdazat. "No," thought the poor lady, "they are all such names!" To satisfy her, they opened the calendar at another place, and the names which turned up were:

*It seemed as though nothing in the world existed for him outside his copying*

Trifily, Dula, Varahasy. "What an infliction!" said the mother. "What names they all are! I really never heard such names. Varadat or Varuh would be bad enough, but Trifily and Varahasy!" They turned over another page and the names were: Pavsikahy and Vahtisy. "Well, I see," said the mother, "it is clear that it is his fate. Since that is how it is, he had better be called after his father, his father is Akaky, let the son be Akaky, too." This was how he came to be Akaky Akakyevitch. The baby was christened and cried and made wry faces during the ceremony, as though he foresaw that he would be a titular councillor. So that was how it all came to pass. We have recalled it here so that the reader may see for himself that it happened quite inevitably and that to give him any other name was out of the question. No one has been able to remember when and how long ago he entered the department, nor who gave him the job. However many directors and higher officials of all sorts came and went, he was always seen in the same place, in the same position, at the very same duty, precisely the same copying clerk, so that they used to declare that he must have been born a copying clerk in uniform all complete and with a bald patch on his head. No respect at all was shown him in the department. The porters, far from getting up from their seats when he came in, took no more notice of him than if a simple fly had flown across the vestibule. His superiors treated him with a sort of domineering chilliness. The head clerk's assistant used to throw papers under his nose without even saying: "Copy this" or "Here is an interesting, nice little case" or some agreeable remark of the sort, as is usually done in well-behaved offices. And he would take it, gazing only at the paper without looking to see who had put it there and whether he had the right to do so; he would take it and at once set to work to copy it. The young clerks jeered and made jokes at him to the best of their clerkly wit, and told before his face all sorts of stories of their own invention about him; they would say of his landlady, an old woman of seventy, that she beat him, would enquire when the wedding was to take place, and would scatter bits of paper on his head, calling them snow. Akaky Akakyevitch never answered a word, however, but behaved as though there were no one there. It had no influence on his work even; in the midst of all this teasing, he never made a single mistake in his copying. Only when the jokes were too unbearable, when they jolted his arm and prevented him from going on with his work, he would bring out: "Leave me alone! Why do you insult me?" and there was something strange in the words and in the voice in which they were uttered. There was a note in it of something that aroused compassion, so that one young man, new to the office, who, following the example of the rest, had allowed himself to mock at him, suddenly stopped as though cut to the heart, and from that time forth, everything was, as it were, changed and appeared in a different light to him. Some unnatural force seemed to thrust him away from the companions with whom he had become acquainted, accepting them as well-bred, polished people. And long afterwards, at moments of the greatest gaiety, the figure of the humble little clerk with a bald patch on his head rose before him with his heart-rending words: "Leave me alone! Why do you insult me?" and in those heart-rending words he heard others: "I am your brother." And the poor young man hid his face in his hands, and many times afterwards in his life he shuddered, seeing how much inhumanity there is in man, how much savage brutality lies hidden under refined, cultured politeness, and, my God! even in a man whom the world accepts as a gentleman and a man of honor. . . .

It would be hard to find a man who lived in his work as did Akaky Akakyevitch. To say that he was zealous in his work is not enough;

no, he loved his work. In it, in that copying, he found a varied and agreeable world of his own. There was a look of enjoyment on his face; certain letters were favorites with him, and when he came to them he was delighted; he chuckled to himself and winked and moved his lips, so that it seemed as though every letter his pen was forming could be read in his face. If rewards had been given according to the measure of zeal in the service, he might to his amazement have even found himself a civil councillor; but all he gained in the service, as the wits, his fellow-clerks, expressed it, was a buckle in his button-hole and a pain in his back. It cannot be said, however, that no notice had ever been taken of him. One director, being a good-natured man and anxious to reward him for his long service, sent him something a little more important than his ordinary copying; he was instructed from a finished document to make some sort of report for another office; the work consisted only of altering the headings and in places changing the first person into the third. This cost him such an effort that it threw him into a regular perspiration: he mopped his brow and said at last, "No, better let me copy something."

From that time forth they left him to go on copying for ever. It seemed as though nothing in the world existed for him outside his copying. He gave no thought at all to his clothes; his uniform was —well, not green but some sort of rusty, muddy color. His collar was very short and narrow, so that, although his neck was not particularly long, yet, standing out of the collar, it looked as immensely long as those of the plaster kittens that wag their heads and are carried about on trays on the heads of dozens of foreigners living in Russia. And there were always things sticking to his uniform, either bits of hay or threads; moreover, he had a special art of passing under a window at the very moment when various rubbish was being flung out into the street, and so was continually carrying off bits of melon rind and similar litter on his hat. He had never once in his life noticed what was being done and going on in the streets, all those things at which, as we all know, his colleagues, the young clerks, always stare, carrying their sharp sight so far even as to notice any one on the other side of the pavement with a trouser strap hanging loose—a detail which always calls forth a sly grin. Whatever Akaky Akakyevitch looked at, he saw nothing anywhere but his clear, evenly written lines, and only perhaps when a horse's head suddenly appeared from nowhere just on his shoulder, and its nostrils blew a perfect gale upon his cheek, did he notice that he was not in the middle of his writing, but rather in the middle of the street.

On reaching home, he would sit down at once to the table, hurriedly sup his soup and eat a piece of beef with an onion; he did not notice the taste at all, but ate it all up together with the flies and anything else that Providence chanced to send him. When he felt that his stomach was beginning to be full, he would rise up from the table, get out a bottle of ink and set to copying the papers he had brought home with him. When he had none to do, he would make a copy expressly for his own pleasure, particularly if the document were remarkable not for the beauty of its style but for the fact of its being addressed to some new or important personage.

Even at those hours when the grey Petersburg sky is completely overcast and the whole population of clerks have dined and eaten their fill, each as best he can, according to the salary he receives and his personal tastes; when they are all resting after the scratching of pens and bustle of the office, their own necessary work and other people's, and all the tasks that an over-zealous man voluntarily sets himself even beyond what is necessary; when the clerks are hastening to devote what is left of their time to pleasure; some more enterprising are flying to the theatre, others to the street to spend their leisure, staring at women's hats, some to spend the evening paying compliments to some attractive girl, the star of a little official circle, while some—and this is the most frequent of all—go simply to a fellow-clerk's flat on the third or fourth storey, two little rooms with an entry or a kitchen, with some pretentions to style, with a lamp or some such article that has cost many sacrifices of dinners and excursions—at the time when all the clerks are scattered about the little flats of their friends, playing a tempestuous game of whist, sipping tea out of glasses to the accompaniment of farthing rusks, sucking in smoke from long pipes, telling, as the cards are dealt, some scandal that has floated down from higher circles, a pleasure which the Russian can never by any possibility deny himself, or, when there is nothing better to talk about, repeating the everlasting anecdote of the commanding officer who was told that the tail had been cut off the horse on the Falconet monument—in short, even when every one was eagerly seeking entertainment, Akaky Akakyevitch did not give himself up to any amusement. No one could say that they had ever seen him at an evening party. After working to his heart's content, he would go to bed, smiling at the thought of the next day and wondering what God would send him to copy. So flowed on the peaceful life of a man who knew how to be content with his fate on a salary of four hundred roubles, and so perhaps it would have flowed on to extreme old age, had it not been for the various calamities that bestrew the path through life, not only of titular, but even of privy, actual court, and all other councillors, even those who neither give council to others nor accept it themselves.

There is in Petersburg a mighty foe of all who receive a salary of four hundred roubles or about that sum. That foe is none other than our northern frost, although it is said to be very good for the health. Between eight and nine in the morning, precisely at the hour when the streets are full of clerks going to their departments, the frost begins giving such sharp and stinging flips at all their noses indiscriminately that the poor fellows don't know what to do with them. At that time, when even those in the higher grade have a pain in their brows and tears in their eyes from the frost, the poor titular councillors are sometimes almost defenseless. Their only protection lies in running as fast as they can through five or six streets in a wretched, thin little overcoat and then warming their feet thoroughly in the porter's room, till all their faculties and qualifications for their various duties thaw again after being frozen on the way. Akaky Akakyevitch had for some time been feeling that his back and shoulders were particularly nipped by the cold, although he did try to run the regular distance as fast as he could. He wondered at last whether there were any defects in his overcoat. After examining it thoroughly in the privacy of his home, he discovered that in two or three places, to wit on the back and the shoulders, it had become a regular sieve; the cloth was so worn that you could see through it and the lining was coming out. I must observe that Akaky Akakyevitch's overcoat had also served as a butt for the jibes of the clerks. It had even been deprived of the honorable name of overcoat and had been referred to as the "dressing jacket." It was indeed of rather a strange make. Its collar had been growing smaller year by year as it served to patch the other parts. The patches were not good specimens of the tailor's art, and they certainly looked clumsy and ugly. On seeing what was wrong, Akaky Akakyevitch decided that he would have to take the overcoat to Petrovitch, a tailor who lived on a fourth storey up a back staircase, and, in spite of having only one eye and being pock-marked all over his face, was rather successful in repairing the trousers and coats of clerks and others—that is, when he was sober, be it understood, and had no other enterprise in his mind. Of this tailor I ought not, of course, to say much, but since it is now the rule that the character of every person in a novel must be completely drawn, well, there is no help for it, here is Petrovitch too. At first he was called simply Grigory, and was a serf belonging to some gentleman or other. He began to be called Petrovitch from the time that he got his freedom and began to drink rather heavily on every holiday, at first only on the chief holidays, but afterwards on all church holidays indiscriminately, wherever there is a cross in the calendar. On that side he was true to the customs of his forefathers, and when he quarrelled with his wife used to call her "a worldly woman and a German." Since we have now mentioned the wife, it will be necessary to say a few words about her too, but unfortunately not much is known about her, except indeed that Petrovitch had a wife and that she wore a cap and not a kerchief, but apparently she could not boast of beauty; anyway, none but soldiers of the Guards peeped under her cap when they met her, and they twitched their moustaches and gave vent to a rather peculiar sound.

As he climbed the stairs, leading to Petrovitch's—which, to do them justice, were all soaked with water and slops and saturated through and through with that smell of spirits which makes the eyes smart, and is, as we all know, inseparable from the back-stairs of Petersburg houses—Akaky Akakyevitch was already wondering how much Petrovitch would ask for the job, and inwardly resolving not to give more than two roubles. The door was open, for Petrovitch's wife was frying some fish and had so filled the kitchen with smoke that you could not even see the black-beetles. Akaky Akakyevitch crossed the kitchen unnoticed by the good woman, and walked

at last into a room where he saw Petrovitch sitting on a big, wooden, unpainted table with his legs tucked under him like a Turkish Pasha. The feet, as is usual with tailors when they sit at work, were bare; and the first object that caught Akaky Akakyevitch's eye was the big toe, with which he was already familiar, with a misshapen nail as thick and strong as the shell of a tortoise. Round Petrovitch's neck hung a skein of silk and another of thread and on his knees was a rag of some sort. He had for the last three minutes been trying to thread his needle, but could not get the thread into the eye and so was very angry with the darkness and indeed with the thread itself, muttering in an undertone: "It won't go in, the savage! You wear me out, you rascal." Akaky Akakyevitch was vexed that he had come just at the minute when Petrovitch was in a bad humor; he liked to give him an order when he was a little "elevated," or, as his wife expressed it, "had fortified himself with fizz, the one-eyed devil." In such circumstances Petrovitch was as a rule very ready to give way and agree, and invariably bowed and thanked him, indeed. Afterwards, it is true, his wife would come wailing that her husband had been drunk and so had asked too little, but adding a single ten-kopeck piece would settle that. But on this occasion Petrovitch was apparently sober and consequently curt, unwilling to bargain, and the devil knows what price he would be ready to lay on. Akaky Akakyevitch perceived this, and was, as the saying is, beating a retreat, but things had gone too far, for Petrovitch was screwing up his solitary eye very attentively at him and Akaky Akakyevitch involuntarily brought out: "Good day, Petrovitch!" "I wish you a good day, sir," said Petrovitch, and squinted at Akaky Akakyevitch's hands, trying to discover what sort of goods he had brought.

"Here I have come to you, Petrovitch, do you see . . . !"

It must be noticed that Akaky Akakyevitch for the most part explained himself by apologies, vague phrases, and particles which have absolutely no significance whatever. If the subject were a very difficult one, it was his habit indeed to leave his sentences quite unfinished, so that very often after a sentence had begun with the words, "It really is, don't you know . . ." nothing at all would follow and he himself would be quite oblivious, supposing he had said all that was necessary.

"What is it?" said Petrovitch, and at the same time with his solitary eye he scrutinized his whole uniform from the collar to the sleeves, the back, the skirts, the button-holes—with all of which he was very familiar, they were all his own work. Such scrutiny is habitual with tailors, it is the first thing they do on meeting one.

"It's like this, Petrovitch . . . the overcoat, the cloth . . . you see everywhere else it is quite strong; it's a little dusty and looks as though it were old, but it is new and it is only in one place just a little . . . on the back, and just a little worn on one shoulder and on this shoulder, too, a little . . . do you see? that's all, and it's not much work. . . ."

Petrovitch took the "dressing jacket," first spread it out over the table, examined it for a long time, shook his head and put his hand out to the window for a round snuff-box with a portrait on the lid of some general—which precisely I can't say, for a finger had been thrust through the spot where a face should have been, and the hole had been pasted up with a square bit of paper. After taking a pinch of snuff, Petrovitch held the "dressing jacket" up in his hands and looked at it against the light, and again he shook his head; then he turned it with the lining upwards and once more shook his head; again he took off the lid with the general pasted up with paper and stuffed a pinch into his nose, shut the box, put it away and at last said: "No, it can't be repaired; a wretched garment!"

"Why can't it, Petrovitch?" he said, almost in the imploring voice of a child. "Why, the only thing is it is a bit worn on the shoulders; why, you have got some little pieces. . . ."

"Yes, the pieces will be found all right," said Petrovitch, "but it can't be patched, the stuff is quite rotten; if you put a needle in it, it would give way."

"Let it give way, but you just put a patch on it."

"There is nothing to put a patch on. There is nothing for it to hold on to; there is a great strain on it, it is not worth calling cloth, it would fly away at a breath of wind."

"Well, then, strengthen it with something—upon my word, really, this is . . . !"

"No," said Petrovitch resolutely, "there is nothing to be done, the thing is no good at all. You had far better, when the cold winter weather comes, make yourself leg wrappings out of it, for there is no warmth in stockings, the Germans invented them just to make money." (Petrovitch was fond of a dig at the Germans occasionally.) "And as for the overcoat, it is clear that you will have to have a new one."

At the word "new" there was a mist before Akaky Akakyevitch's eyes, and everything in the room seemed blurred. He could see nothing clearly but the general with the piece of paper over his face on the lid of Petrovitch's snuff-box.

"A new one?" he said, still feeling as though he were in a dream; "why, I haven't the money for it."

"Yes, a new one," Petrovitch repeated with barbarous composure.

"Well, and if I did have a new one, how much would it . . . ?"

"You mean what will it cost?"

"Yes."

"Well, three fifty-rouble notes or more," said Petrovitch, and he compressed his lips significantly. He was very fond of making an effect, he was fond of suddenly disconcerting a man completely and then squinting sideways to see what sort of a face he made.

---

"A hundred and fifty roubles for an overcoat," screamed poor Akaky Akakyevitch—it was perhaps the first time he had screamed in his life, for he was always distinguished by the softness of his voice.

"Yes," said Petrovitch, "and even then it's according to the coat. If I were to put marten on the collar, and add a hood with silk linings, it would come to two hundred."

"Petrovitch, please," said Akaky Akakyevitch in an imploring voice, not hearing and not trying to hear what Petrovitch said, and missing all his effects, "do repair it somehow, so that it will serve a little longer."

"No, that would be wasting work and spending money for nothing," said Petrovitch, and after that Akaky Akakyevitch went away completely crushed, and when he had gone Petrovitch remained standing for a long time with his lips pursed up significantly before he took up his work again, feeling pleased that he had not demeaned himself nor lowered the dignity of the tailor's art.

When he got into the street, Akaky Akakyevitch was as though in a dream. "So that is how it is," he said to himself. "I really did not think it would be so . . ." and then after a pause he added, "So there it is! so that's how it is at last! and I really could never have supposed it would have been so. And there . . ." There followed another long silence, after which he brought out: "So there it is! well, it really is so utterly unexpected . . . who would have thought . . . what a circumstance. . . ." Saying this, instead of going home he walked off in quite the opposite direction without suspecting what he was doing. On the way a clumsy sweep brushed the whole of his sooty side against him and blackened all his shoulder; a regular hatful of plaster scattered upon him from the top of a house that was being built. He noticed nothing of this, and only after he had jostled against a sentry who had set his halberd down beside him and was shaking some snuff out of his horn into his rough fist, he came to himself a little and then only because the sentry said: "Why are you poking yourself right in one's face, haven't you the pavement to yourself?" This made him look round and turn homeward; only there he began to collect his thoughts, to see his position in a clear and true light and began talking to himself no longer incoherently but reasonably and openly as with a sensible friend with whom one can discuss the most intimate and vital matters. "No, indeed," said Akaky Akakyevitch, "it is no use talking to Petrovitch now; just now he really is . . . his wife must have been giving it to him. I had better go to him on Sunday morning; after the Saturday evening he will be squinting and sleepy, so he'll want a little drink to carry it off and his wife won't give him a penny. I'll slip ten kopecks into his hand and then he will be more accommodating and maybe take the overcoat. . . ."

So reasoning with himself, Akaky Akakyevitch cheered up and waited until the next Sunday; then, seeing from a distance Petrovitch's wife leaving the house, he went straight in. Petrovitch certainly was very tipsy after the Saturday. He could hardly hold his head up and was very drowsy: but, for all that, as soon as he heard what he was speaking about, it seemed as though the devil had nudged him. "I can't," he said, "you must kindly order a new one." Akaky Akakyevitch at once slipped a ten-kopeck piece into his hand. "I thank you, sir, I will have just a drop to your health, but don't trouble yourself about the overcoat; it is not a bit of good for anything. I'll make you a fine new coat, you can trust me for that."

Akaky Akakyevitch would have said more about repairs, but Petrovitch, without listening, said: "A new one now I'll make you without fail; you can rely upon that, I'll do my best. It could even be like the fashion that has come in with the collar to button with silver claws under appliqué."

Then Akaky Akakyevitch saw that there was no escape from a new overcoat and he was utterly depressed. How indeed, for what, with what money could he get it? Of course he could to some extent rely on the bonus for the coming holiday, but that money had long ago been appropriated and its use determined beforehand. It was needed for new trousers and to pay the cobbler an old debt for putting some new tops to some old boot-legs, and he had to order three shirts from a seamstress as well as two specimens of an undergarment which it is improper to mention in print; in short, all that money absolutely must be spent, and even if the director were to be so gracious as to assign him a gratuity of forty-five or even fifty, instead of forty roubles, there would be still left a mere trifle, which would be but as a drop in the ocean beside the fortune needed for an overcoat. Though, of course, he knew that Petrovitch had a strange craze for suddenly putting on the devil knows what enormous price, so that at times his own wife could not help crying out: "Why, you are out of your wits, you idiot! Another time he'll undertake a job for nothing, and here the devil has bewitched him to ask more than he is worth himself." Though, of course, he knew that Petrovitch would undertake to make it for eighty roubles, still where would he get those eighty roubles? He might manage half of that sum; half of it could be found, perhaps even a little more; but where could he get the other half? . . . But, first of all, the reader ought to know where that first half was to be found. Akaky Akakyevitch had the habit every time he spent a rouble of putting aside two kopecks in a little locked-up box with a slit in the lid for slipping the money in. At the end of every half-year he would inspect the pile of coppers there and change them for small silver. He had done this for a long time, and in the course of many years the sum had mounted up to forty roubles and so he had half the money in his hands, but where was he to get the other half, where was he to get another forty roubles? Akaky Akakyevitch pondered and pondered and decided at last that he would have to diminish his ordinary expenses, at least for a year; give up burning candles in the evening, and if he had to do anything he must go into the landlady's room and work by her candle; that as he walked along the streets he must walk as lightly and carefully as possible, almost on tiptoe, on the cobbles and flagstones, so that his soles might last a little longer than usual; that he must send his linen to the wash less frequently, and that, to preserve it from being worn, he must take it off every day when he came home and sit in a thin cotton-shoddy dressing-gown, a very ancient garment which Time itself had spared. To tell the truth, he found it at first rather hard to get used to these privations, but after a while it became a habit and went smoothly enough—he even became quite accustomed to being hungry in the evening; on the other hand, he had spiritual nourishment, for he carried ever in his thoughts the idea of his future overcoat. His whole existence had in a sense become fuller, as though he had married, as though some other person were present with him, as though he were no longer alone, but an agreeable companion had consented to walk the path of life hand in hand with him, and that companion was no other than the new overcoat with its thick wadding and its strong, durable lining. He became, as it were, more alive, even more strong-willed, like a man who has set before himself a definite aim. Uncertainty, indecision, in fact all the hesitating and vague characteristics vanished from his face and his manners. At times there was a gleam in his eyes, indeed, the most bold and audacious ideas flashed through his mind. Why not really have marten on the collar? Meditation on the subject always made him absent-minded. On one occasion when he was copying a document, he very nearly made a mistake, so that he almost cried out "ough" aloud and crossed himself. At least once every month he went to Petrovitch to talk about the overcoat, where it would be best to buy the cloth, and what color it should be, and what price, and, though he returned home a little anxious, he was always pleased at the thought that at last the time was at hand when everything would be bought and the overcoat would be made. Things moved even faster than he had anticipated. Contrary to all expectations, the director bestowed on Akaky Akakyevitch a gratuity of no less than sixty roubles. Whether it was that he had an inkling that Akaky Akakyevitch needed a greatcoat, or whether it happened so by chance, owing to this he found he had twenty roubles extra. This circumstance hastened the course of affairs. Another two or three months of partial fasting and Akaky Akakyevitch had actually saved up nearly eighty roubles. His heart, as a rule very tranquil, began to throb. The very first day he set off in company with Petrovitch to the shops. They bought some very good cloth, and no wonder, since they had been thinking of it for more than six months before, and scarcely a month had passed without their going to the shop to compare prices; now Petrovitch himself declared that there was no better cloth to be had. For the lining they chose calico, but of a stout quality, which in Petrovich's words was even better than silk, and actually as strong and handsome to look at. Marten they did not buy, because it certainly was dear, but instead they chose cat fur, the best to be found in the shop—cat which in the distance might almost be taken for marten. Petrovitch was busy over the coat for a whole fortnight, because there were a great many button-holes, otherwise it would have been ready sooner. Petrovitch asked twelve roubles for the work; less than that it hardly could have been, every-

THE OVERCOAT

thing was sewn with silk, with fine double seams, and Petrovitch
went over every seam afterwards with his own teeth imprinting various figures with them. It was . . . it is hard to say precisely on what
day, but probably on the most triumphant day of the life of Akaky
Akakyevitch that Petrovitch at last brought the overcoat. He
brought it in the morning, just before it was time to set off for the
department. The overcoat could not have arrived more in the nick
of time, for rather sharp frosts were just beginning and seemed
threatening to be even more severe. Petrovitch brought the greatcoat himself as a good tailor should. There was an expression of importance on his face, such as Akaky Akakyevitch had never seen
there before. He seemed fully conscious of having completed a work
of no little moment and of having shown in his own person the gulf
that separates tailors who only put in linings and do repairs from
those who make up new materials. He took the greatcoat out of the
bandana in which he had brought it (the bandana had just come
home from the wash), he then folded it up and put it in his pocket
for future use. After taking out the overcoat, he looked at it with
much pride and, holding it in both hands, threw it very deftly over
Akaky Akakyevitch's shoulders, then pulled it down and smoothed
it out behind with his hands; then draped it about Akaky Akakyevitch with somewhat jaunty carelessness. The latter, as a man advanced in years, wished to try it with his arms in the sleeves. Petrovitch helped him to put it on, and it appeared that it looked splendid
too with his arms in the sleeves. In fact it turned out that the overcoat was completely and entirely successful. Petrovitch did not let
slip the occasion for observing that it was only because he lived in
a small street and had no signboard, and because he had known
Akaky Akakyevitch so long, that he had done it so cheaply, but on
the Nevsky Prospect they would have asked him seventy-five roubles

for the work alone. Akaky Akakyevitch had no inclination to discuss this with Petrovitch, besides he was frightened of the big sums that Petrovitch was fond of flinging airily about in conversation. He paid him, thanked him, and went off on the spot, with his new overcoat on, to the department. Petrovitch followed him out and stopped in the street, staring for a good time at the coat from a distance and then purposely turned off and, taking a short cut by a side street, came back into the street and got another view of the coat from the other side, that is, from the front.

Meanwhile Akaky Akakyevitch walked along with every emotion in its most holiday mood. He felt every second that he had a new overcoat on his shoulders, and several times he actually laughed from inward satisfaction. Indeed, it had two advantages, one that it was warm and the other that it was good. He did not notice the way at all and found himself all at once at the department; in the porter's room he took off the overcoat, looked it over and put it in the porter's special care. I cannot tell how it happened, but all at once every one in the department learned that Akaky Akakyevitch had a new overcoat and that the "dressing jacket" no longer existed. They all ran out at once into the porter's room to look at Akaky Akakyevitch's new overcoat, they began welcoming him and congratulating him so that at first he could do nothing but smile and afterwards felt positively abashed. When, coming up to him, they all began saying that he must "sprinkle" the new overcoat and that he ought at least to stand them all a supper, Akaky Akakyevitch lost his head completely and did not know what to do, how to get out of it, nor what to answer. A few minutes later, flushing crimson, he even began assuring them with great simplicity that it was not a new overcoat at all, that it was just nothing, that it was an old overcoat. At last one of the clerks, indeed the assistant of the head clerk of the room, probably in order to show that he was not proud and was able to get on with those beneath him, said: "So be it, I'll give a party instead of Akaky Akakyevitch and invite you all to tea with me this evening; as luck would have it, it is my name-day." The clerks naturally congratulated the assistant head clerk and eagerly accepted the invitation. Akaky Akakyevitch was beginning to make excuses, but they all declared that it was uncivil of him, that it was simply a shame and a disgrace and that he could not possibly refuse. However, he felt pleased about it afterwards when he remembered that through this he would have the opportunity of going out in the evening, too, in his new overcoat. That whole day was for Akaky Akakyevitch the most triumphant and festive day in his life. He returned home in the happiest frame of mind, took off the overcoat and hung it carefully on the wall, admiring the cloth and lining once more, and then pulled out his old "dressing jacket," now completely coming to pieces, on purpose to compare them. He glanced at it and positively laughed, the difference was so immense! And long afterwards he went on laughing at dinner, as the position in which the "dressing jacket" was placed recurred to his mind. He dined in excellent spirits and after dinner wrote nothing, no papers at all, but just took his ease for a little while on his bed, till it got dark, then, without putting things off, he dressed, put on his overcoat, and went out into the street. Where precisely the clerk who had invited him lived we regret to say that we cannot tell; our memory is beginning to fail sadly, and everything there is in Petersburg, all the streets and houses, are so blurred and muddled in our head that it is a very difficult business to put anything in orderly fashion. However that may have been, there is no doubt that the clerk lived in the better part of the town and consequently a very long distance from Akaky Akakyevitch. At first the latter had to walk through deserted streets, scantily lighted, but as he approached his destination the streets became more lively, more full of people, and more brightly lighted; passers-by began to be more frequent, ladies began to appear, here and there, beautifully dressed, beaver collars were to be seen on the men. Cabmen with wooden trellis-work sledges, studded with gilt nails, were less frequently to be met; on the other hand, jaunty drivers in raspberry colored velvet caps with varnished sledges and bearskin rugs appeared, and carriages with decorated boxes dashed along the streets, their wheels crunching through the snow.

Akaky Akakyevitch looked at all this as a novelty; for several years he had not gone out into the streets in the evening. He stopped with curiosity before a lighted shop-window to look at a picture in which a beautiful woman was represented in the act of taking off her shoe and displaying as she did so the whole of a very shapely leg, while behind her back a gentleman with whiskers and a handsome imperial on his chin was putting his head in at the door. Akaky Akakyevitch shook his head and smiled and then went on his way. Why did he smile? Was it because he had come across something quite unfamiliar to him, though every man retains some instinctive feeling on the subject, or was it that he reflected, like many other clerks, as follows: "Well, upon my soul, those Frenchmen! it's beyond anything! if they try anything of the sort, it really is . . . !" Though possibly he did not even think that; there is no creeping into a man's soul and finding out all that he thinks. At last he reached the house in which the assistant head clerk lived in fine style; there was a lamp burning on the stairs, and the flat was on the second floor. As he went into the entry Akaky Akakyevitch saw whole rows of goloshes. Amongst them in the middle of the room stood a samovar hissing and letting off clouds of steam. On the walls hung coats and cloaks, among which some actually had beaver collars or velvet

revers. The other side of the wall there was noise and talk, which suddenly became clear and loud when the door opened and the footman came out with a tray full of empty glasses, a jug of cream, and a basket of biscuits. It was evident that the clerks had arrived long before and had already drunk their first glass of tea. Akaky Akakyevitch, after hanging up his coat with his own hands, went into the room, and at the same moment there flashed before his eyes a vision of candles, clerks, pipes, and card tables, together with the confused sounds of conversation rising up on all sides and the noise of moving chairs. He stopped very awkwardly in the middle of the room, looking about and trying to think what to do, but he was observed and received with a shout and they all went at once into the entry and again took a look at his overcoat. Though Akaky Akakyevitch was somewhat embarrassed, yet, being a simple-hearted man, he could not help being pleased at seeing how they all admired his coat. Then of course they all abandoned him and his coat, and turned their attention as usual to the tables set for whist. All this—the noise, the talk, and the crowd of people—was strange and wonderful to Akaky Akakyevitch. He simply did not know how to behave, what to do with his arms and legs and his whole figure; at last he sat down beside the players, looked at the cards, stared first at one and then at another of the faces, and in a little while began to yawn and felt that he was bored—especially as it was long past the time at which he usually went to bed. He tried to take leave of his hosts, but they would not let him go, saying that he absolutely must have a glass of champagne in honor of the new coat. An hour later supper was served, consisting of salad, cold veal, a pasty, pies, and tarts from the confectioner's, and champagne. They made Akaky Akakyevitch drink two glasses, after which he felt that things were much more cheerful, though he could not forget that it was twelve o'clock and that he ought to have been home long ago. That his host might not take it into his head to detain him, he slipped out of the room, hunted in the entry for his greatcoat, which he found, not without regret, lying on the floor, shook it, removed some fluff from it, put it on, and went down the stairs into the street. It was still light in the streets. Some little general shops, those perpetual clubs for house-serfs and all sorts of people, were open; others which were closed showed, however, a long streak of light at every crack of the door, proving that they were not yet deserted, and probably maids and men-servants were still finishing their conversation and discussion, driving their masters to utter perplexity as to their whereabouts. Akaky Akakyevitch walked along in a cheerful state of mind; he was even on the point of running, goodness knows why, after a lady of some sort who passed by like lightning with every part of her frame in violent motion. He checked himself at once, however, and again walked along very gently, feeling positively surprised himself at the inexplicable impulse that had seized him. Soon the deserted streets, which are not particularly cheerful by day and even less so in the evening, stretched before him. Now they were still more dead and deserted; the light of street lamps was scantier, the oil was evidently running low; then came wooden houses and fences; not a soul anywhere; only the snow gleamed on the streets and the low-pitched slumbering hovels looked black and gloomy with their closed shutters. He approached the spot where the street was intersected by an endless square, which looked like a fearful desert with its houses scarcely visible on the further side.

In the distance, goodness knows where, there was a gleam of light from some sentry-box which seemed to be standing at the end of the world. Akaky Akakyevitch's light-heartedness grew somehow sensibly less at this place. He stepped into the square, not without an involuntary uneasiness, as though his heart had a foreboding of evil. He looked behind him and to both sides—it was as though the sea were all round him. "No, better not look," he thought, and walked on, shutting his eyes, and when he opened them to see whether the end of the square were near, he suddenly saw standing before him, almost under his very nose, some men with moustaches; just what they were like he could not even distinguish. There was a mist before his eyes and a throbbing in his chest. "I say the overcoat is mine!" said one of them in a voice like a clap of thunder, seizing him by the collar. Akaky Akakyevitch was on the point of shouting "Help" when another put a fist the size of a clerk's head against his very lips, saying: "You just shout now." Akaky Akakyevitch felt only that they took the overcoat off, and gave him a kick with their knees, and he fell on his face in the snow and was conscious of nothing more. A few minutes later he came to himself and got on to his feet, but there was no one there. He felt that it was cold on the ground and that he had no overcoat, and began screaming, but it seemed as though his voice could not carry to the end of the square. Overwhelmed with despair and continuing to scream, he ran across the square straight to the sentry-box, beside which stood a sentry leaning on his halberd and, so it seemed, looking with curiosity to see who the devil the man was who was screaming and running towards him from the distance. As Akaky Akakyevitch reached him, he began breathlessly shouting that he was asleep and not looking after his duty not to see that a man was being robbed. The sentry answered that he had seen nothing, that he had only seen him stopped in the middle of the square by two men, and supposed that they were his friends, and that, instead of abusing him for nothing, he had better go the next day to the superintendent and that he would find out who had taken the overcoat. Akaky Akakyevitch ran

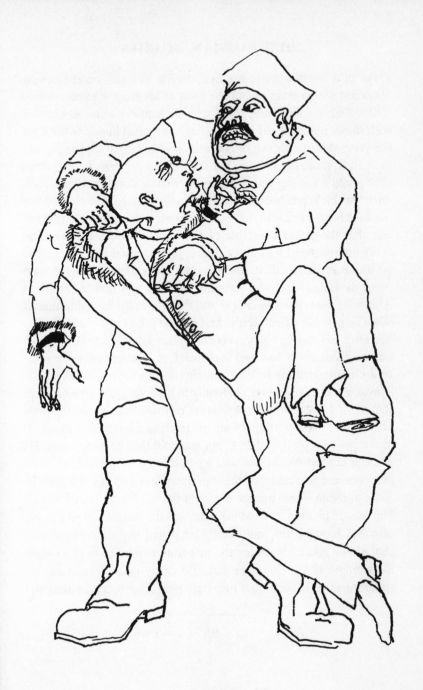

home in a terrible state: his hair, which was still comparatively abundant on his temples and the back of his head, was completely dishevelled; his sides and chest and his trousers were all covered with snow. When his old landlady heard a fearful knock at the door she jumped hurriedly out of bed and, with only one slipper on, ran to open it, modestly holding her shift across her bosom; but when she opened it she stepped back, seeing what a state Akaky Akakye-vitch was in. When he told her what had happened, she clasped her hands in horror and said that he must go straight to the superintend-ent, that the police constable of the quarter would deceive him, make promises and lead him a dance; that it would be best of all to go to the superintendent, and that she knew him indeed, because Anna the Finnish girl who was once her cook was now in service as a nurse at the superintendent's; and that she often saw him himself when he passed by their house, and that he used to be every Sunday at church too, saying his prayers and at the same time looking good-humoredly at every one, and that therefore by every token he must be a kind-hearted man. After listening to this advice, Akaky Aka-kyevitch made his way very gloomily to his room, and how he spent that night I leave to the imagination of those who are in the least able to picture the position of others. Early in the morning he set off to the police superintendent's, but was told that he was asleep. He came at ten o'clock, he was told again that he was asleep; he came at eleven and was told that the superintendent was not at home; he came at dinner-time, but the clerks in the ante-room would not let him in, and insisted on knowing what was the matter and what busi-ness had brought him and exactly what had happened; so that at last Akaky Akakyevitch for the first time in his life tried to show the strength of his character and said curtly that he must see the superintendent himself, that they dare not refuse to admit him, that he had come from the department on government business, and that if he made complaint of them they would see. The clerks dared say nothing to this, and one of them went to summon the superintendent. The latter received his story of being robbed of his overcoat in an extremely strange way. Instead of attending to the main point, he began asking Akaky Akakyevitch questions, why had he been coming home so late? wasn't he going, or hadn't he been, to some house of ill-fame? so that Akaky Akakyevitch was overwhelmed with confusion, and went away without knowing whether or not the proper measures would be taken in regard to his overcoat. He was absent from the office all that day (the only time that it had happened in his life). Next day he appeared with a pale face, wearing his old "dressing jacket" which had become a still more pitiful sight. The tidings of the theft of the overcoat—though there were clerks who did not let even this chance slip of jeering at Akaky Akakyevitch—touched many of them. They decided on the spot to get up a subscription for him, but collected only a very trifling sum, because the clerks had already spent a good deal on subscribing to the director's portrait and on the purchase of a book, at the suggestion of the head of their department, who was a friend of the author, and so the total realized was very insignificant. One of the clerks, moved by compassion, ventured at any rate to assist Akaky Akakyevitch with good advice, telling him not to go to the district police inspector, because, though it might happen that the latter might be sufficiently zealous of gaining the approval of his superiors to succeed in finding the overcoat, it would remain in the possession of the police unless he presented legal proofs that it belonged to him; he urged that far the best thing would be to appeal to a Person of Consequence; that the Person of Consequence, by writing and getting into communication with the proper authorities, could push the matter through more successfully. There was nothing else for it. Akaky Akakyevitch made up his mind to go to the Person of Consequence. What precisely was the nature of the functions of the Person of Consequence has remained a matter of uncertainty. It must be noted that this Person of Consequence had only lately become a person of consequence, and until recently had been a person of no consequence. Though, indeed, his position even now was not reckoned of consequence in comparison with others of still greater consequence. But there is always to be found a circle of persons to whom a person of little consequence in the eyes of others is a person of consequence. It is true that he did his utmost to increase the consequence of his position in various ways, for instance by insisting that his subordinates should come out on to the stairs to meet him when he arrived at his office; that no one should venture to approach him directly but all proceedings should be by the strictest order of precedence, that a collegiate registration clerk should report the matter to the provincial secretary, and the provincial secretary to the titular councillor or whomsoever it might be, and that business should only reach him by this channel. Every one in Holy Russia has a craze for imitation, every one apes and mimics his superiors. I have actually been told that a titular councillor who was put in charge of a small separate office, immediately partitioned off a special room for himself, calling it the head office, and set special porters at the door with red collars and gold lace, who took hold of the handle of the door and opened it for every one who went in, though the "head office" was so tiny that it was with difficulty that an ordinary writing table could be put into it. The manners and habits of the Person of Consequence were dignified and majestic, but not complex. The chief foundation of his system was strictness, "strictness, strictness, and—strictness!" he used to say, and at the last word he would look very significantly at the person he was addressing, though, indeed, he had no reason to do so, for the dozen clerks who made up the whole administrative mechanism of his office stood in befitting awe of him; any clerk who saw him in the distance would leave his work and remain standing at attention till his superior had left the room. His conversation with his subordinates was usually marked by severity and almost confined to three phrases: "How dare you? Do you know to whom you are speaking? Do you understand who I am?" He was, however, at heart a good-natured man, pleasant and obliging with his colleagues; but the grade of general had completely turned his head. When he received it, he was perplexed, thrown off his balance, and quite at a loss how to behave. If he chanced to be with his equals, he was still quite a decent man, a very gentlemanly man, in fact, and in many ways even an intelligent man, but as soon as he was in company with men who were even one grade below him, there was simply no doing anything with him: he sat silent and his position excited compassion, the more so as he himself felt that he might have been spending his time to incomparably more advantage. At times there could be seen in his eyes an intense desire to join in some interesting conversation, but he was restrained by the doubt whether it would not be too much on his part, whether it would not be too great a familiarity and lowering of his dignity, and in consequence of these reflections he remained everlastingly in the same mute condition, only uttering from time to time monosyllabic sounds, and in this way he gained the reputation of being a very tiresome man.

So this was the Person of Consequence to whom our friend Akaky Akakyevitch appealed, and he appealed to him at a most unpropitious moment, very unfortunate for himself, though fortunate, indeed, for the Person of Consequence. The latter happened to be in his study, talking in the very best of spirits with an old friend of his childhood who had only just arrived and whom he had not seen for several years. It was at this moment that he was informed that a man called Bashmatchkin was asking to see him. He asked abruptly, "What sort of man is he?" and received the answer, "A government clerk." "Ah! he can wait, I haven't time now," said the Person of Consequence. Here I must observe that this was a complete lie on the part of the Person of Consequence: he had time; his friend and he had long ago said all they had to say to each other and their conversation had begun to be broken by very long pauses during which they merely slapped each other on the knee, saying, "So that's how things are, Ivan Abramovitch!"—"There it is, Stepan Varlamovitch!" but, for all that, he told the clerk to wait in order to show his friend, who had left the service years before and was living at home in the country, how long clerks had to wait in his ante-room. At last after they had talked, or rather been silent to their heart's content and had smoked a cigar in very comfortable arm-chairs with sloping backs, he seemed suddenly to recollect, and said to the secretary, who was standing at the door with papers for his signature: "Oh, by the way, there is a clerk waiting, isn't there? tell him he can come in." When he saw Akaky Akakyevitch's meek appearance and old uniform, he turned to him at once and said: "What do you want?" in a firm and abrupt voice, which he had purposely practiced in his own room in solitude before the looking-glass for a week before receiving his present post and the grade of a general. Akaky Akakyevitch, who was overwhelmed with befitting awe beforehand, was somewhat confused and, as far as his tongue would allow him, explained to the best of his powers, with even more frequent "ers" than usual, that he had had a perfectly new overcoat and now he had been robbed of it in the most inhuman way, and that now he had come to beg him by his intervention either to correspond with his honor the head policemaster or anybody else, and find the overcoat. This mode of proceeding struck the general for some reason as taking a great liberty. "What next, sir," he went on as abruptly, "don't you know the way to proceed? To whom are you addressing yourself? Don't you know how things are done? You ought first to have handed in a petition to the office; it would have gone to the head clerk of the room, and to the head clerk of the section, then it would have been handed to the secretary and the secretary would have brought it to me. . . ."

"But, your Excellency," said Akaky Akakyevitch, trying to collect all the small allowance of presence of mind he possessed and feeling at the same time that he was getting into a terrible perspiration, "I ventured, your Excellency, to trouble you because secretaries . . . er . . . are people you can't depend on. . . ."

"What? what? what?" said the Person of Consequence, "where did you get hold of that spirit? where did you pick up such ideas? What insubordination is spreading among young men against their superiors and betters." The Person of Consequence did not apparently observe that Akaky Akakyevitch was well over fifty, and therefore if he could have been called a young man it would only have been in comparison with a man of seventy. "Do you know to whom you are speaking? do you understand who I am? do you understand that, I ask you?" At this point he stamped, and raised his voice to such a powerful note that Akaky Akakyevitch was not the only one to be terrified. Akaky Akakyevitch was positively petrified; he staggered, trembling all over, and could not stand; if the porters had not run up to support him, he would have flopped upon the floor; he was led out almost unconscious. The Person of Consequence, pleased that the effect had surpassed his expectations and enchanted at the idea that his words could even deprive a man of consciousness, stole a sideway glance at his friend to see how he was taking it, and perceived not without satisfaction that his friend was feeling very uncertain and even beginning to be a little terrified himself.

How he got downstairs, how he went out into the street—of all that Akaky Akakyevitch remembered nothing, he had no feeling in his arms or his legs. In all his life he had never been so severely reprimanded by a general, and this was by one of another department, too. He went out into the snowstorm, that was whistling through the streets, with his mouth open, and as he went he stumbled off the pavement; the wind, as its way is in Petersburg, blew upon him from all points of the compass and from every side street. In an instant it had blown a quinsy into his throat, and when he got home he was not able to utter a word; with a swollen face and throat he went to bed. So violent is sometimes the effect of a suitable reprimand!

Next day he was in a high fever. Thanks to the gracious assistance of the Petersburg climate, the disease made more rapid progress than could have been expected, and when the doctor came, after feeling his pulse he could find nothing to do but prescribe a fomentation, and that simply that the patient might not be left without the benefit of medical assistance; however, two days later he informed him that his end was at hand, after which he turned to his landlady and said: "And you had better lose no time, my good woman, but order him now a deal coffin—an oak one will be too dear for him." Whether Akaky Akakyevitch heard these fateful words or not, whether they produced a shattering effect upon him, and whether he regretted his pitiful life, no one can tell, for he was all the time in delirium and fever. Apparitions, each stranger than the one before, were continually haunting him: first, he saw Petrovitch and was ordering him to make a greatcoat trimmed with some sort of traps for robbers, who were, he fancied, continually under the bed, and he was calling his landlady every minute to pull out a thief who had even got under the quilt; then he kept asking why his old "dressing jacket" was hanging before him when he had a new overcoat, then he fancied he was standing before the general listening to the appropriate reprimand and saying "I am sorry, your Excellency," then finally he became abusive, uttering the most awful language, so that his old landlady positively crossed herself, having never heard anything of the kind from him before, and the more horrified because these dreadful words followed immediately upon the phrase "your Excellency." Later on, his talk was a mere medley of nonsense, so that it was quite unintelligible; all that could be seen was that his incoherent words and thoughts were concerned with nothing but the overcoat. At last poor Akaky Akakyevitch gave up the ghost. No seal was put upon his room nor upon his things, because, in the first place, he had no heirs and, in the second, the property left was very small, to wit, a bundle of goose-feathers, a quire of white government paper, three pairs of socks, two or three buttons that had come off his trousers, and the "dressing jacket" with which the reader is already familiar. Who came into all this wealth God only knows, even I who tell the tale must own that I have not troubled to inquire. And Petersburg remained without Akaky Akakyevitch, as though, indeed, he had never been in the city. A creature had vanished and departed whose cause no one had championed, who was dear to no one, of interest to no one, who never even attracted the attention of the student of natural history, though the latter does not disdain to fix a common fly upon a pin and look at him under the microscope —a creature who bore patiently the jeers of the office and for no particular reason went to his grave, though even he at the very end of his life was visited by a gleam of brightness in the form of an overcoat that for one instant brought color into his poor life—a creature on whom calamity broke as insufferably as it breaks upon the heads of the mighty ones of this world . . . !

Several days after his death, the porter from the department was sent to his lodgings with instructions that he should go at once to the office, for his chief was asking for him; but the porter was obliged to return without him, explaining that he could not come, and to the inquiry "Why?" he added, "Well, you see: the fact is he is dead, he was buried three days ago." This was how they learned at the office of the death of Akaky Akakyevitch, and the next day there was sitting in his seat a new clerk who was very much taller and who wrote not in the same upright hand but made his letters more slanting and crooked.

But who could have imagined that this was not all there was to tell about Akaky Akakyevitch, that he was destined for a few days to make a noise in the world after his death, as though to make up for his life having been unnoticed by any one? But so it happened, and our poor story unexpectedly finishes with a fantastic ending. Rumors were suddenly floating about Petersburg that in the neighborhood of the Kalinkin Bridge and for a little distance beyond, a corpse had taken to appearing at night in the form of a clerk looking for a stolen overcoat, and stripping from the shoulders of all passersby, regardless of grade and calling, overcoats of all descriptions—trimmed with cat fur or beaver or wadded, lined with raccoon, fox, and bear—made, in fact, of all sorts of skin which men have adapted for the covering of their own. One of the clerks of the department saw the corpse with his own eyes and at once recognized it as Akaky Akakyevitch; but it excited in him such terror, however, that he ran away as fast as his legs could carry him and so could not get a very clear view of him, and only saw him hold up his finger threateningly in the distance.

From all sides complaints were continually coming that backs and shoulders, not of mere titular councillors, but even of upper court councillors, had been exposed to taking chills, owing to being stripped of their greatcoats. Orders were given to the police to catch the corpse regardless of trouble or expense, alive or dead, and to punish him in the cruelest way, as an example to others, and, indeed, they very nearly succeeded in doing so. The sentry of one district police station in Kiryushkin Place snatched a corpse by the collar on the spot of the crime in the very act of attempting to snatch a frieze overcoat from a retired musician, who used in his day to play the flute. Having caught him by the collar, he shouted until he had brought two other comrades, whom he charged to hold him while he felt just a minute in his boot to get out a snuff-box in order to revive his nose which had six times in his life been frost-bitten, but the snuff was probably so strong that not even a dead man could stand it. The sentry had hardly had time to put his finger over his right nostril and draw up some snuff in the left when the corpse sneezed violently right into the eyes of all three. While they were putting their fists up to wipe them, the corpse completely vanished, so that they were not even sure whether he had actually been in their hands. From that time forward, the sentries conceived such a horror of the dead that they were even afraid to seize the living and confined themselves to shouting from the distance: "Hi, you there, be off!" and the dead clerk began to appear even on the other side of the Kalinkin Bridge, rousing no little terror in all timid people.

We have, however, quite deserted the Person of Consequence, who may in reality almost be said to be the cause of the fantastic ending of this perfectly true story. To begin with, my duty requires me to do justice to the Person of Consequence by recording that soon after poor Akaky Akakyevitch had gone away crushed to powder, he felt something not unlike regret. Sympathy was a feeling not unknown to him; his heart was open to many kindly impulses, although his exalted grade very often prevented them from being shown. As soon as his friend had gone out of his study, he even began brooding over poor Akaky Akakyevitch, and from that time forward, he was almost every day haunted by the image of the poor clerk who had succumbed so completely to the befitting reprimand. The thought of the man so worried him that a week later he actually decided to send a clerk to find out how he was and whether he really could help him in any way. And when they brought him word that Akaky Akakyevitch had died suddenly in delirium and fever, it made a great impression on him, his conscience reproached him and he was depressed all day. Anxious to distract his mind and to forget the unpleasant impression, he went to spend the evening with one of his friends, where he found a genteel company and, what was best of all, almost every one was of the same grade so that he was able to be quite free from restraint. This had a wonderful effect on his spirits, he expanded, became affable and genial—in short, spent a very agreeable evening. At supper he drank a couple of glasses of champagne—a proceeding which we all know has a happy effect in inducing good-humor. The champagne made him inclined to do something unusual, and he decided not to go home yet but to visit a lady of his acquaintance, one Karolina Ivanovna—a lady apparently of German extraction, for whom he entertained extremely friendly feelings. It must be noted that the Person of Consequence was a man no longer young, an excellent husband, and the respectable father of a family. He had two sons, one already serving in his office, and a nice-looking daughter of sixteen with a rather turned-up, pretty little nose, who used to come every morning to kiss his hand, saying: *"Bonjour, Papa."* His wife, who was still blooming and decidedly good-looking, indeed, used first to give him her hand

*The clerk's face was white as snow and looked like that of a corpse*

to kiss and then would kiss his hand, turning it the other side up-wards. But though the Person of Consequence was perfectly satisfied with the kind amenities of his domestic life, he thought it proper to have a lady friend in another quarter of the town. This lady friend was not a bit better looking nor younger than his wife, but these mysterious facts exist in the world and it is not our business to criti-cize them. And so the Person of Consequence went downstairs, got into his sledge, and said to his coachman, "To Karolina Ivanovna," while luxuriously wrapped in his warm fur coat he remained in that agreeable frame of mind sweeter to a Russian than anything that could be invented, that is, when one thinks of nothing while thoughts come into the mind of themselves, one pleasanter than the other, without the labor of following them or looking for them. Full of satisfaction, he recalled all the amusing moments of the evening he had spent, all the phrases that had set the little circle laughing; many of them he repeated in an undertone and found them as amus-ing as before, and so, very naturally, laughed very heartily at them again. From time to time, however, he was disturbed by a gust of wind which, blowing suddenly, God knows whence and wherefore, cut him in the face, pelting him with flakes of snow, puffing out his coat-collar like a sack, or suddenly flinging it with unnatural force over his head and giving him endless trouble to extricate himself from it. All at once, the Person of Consequence felt that someone had clutched him very tightly by the collar. Turning round he saw a short man in a shabby old uniform, and not without horror recog-nized him as Akaky Akakyevitch. The clerk's face was white as snow and looked like that of a corpse, but the horror of the Person of Consequence was beyond all bounds when he saw the mouth of the corpse distorted into speech and, breathing upon him the chill of the grave, it uttered the following words: "Ah, so here you are at last! At last I've . . . er . . . caught you by the collar. It's your over-coat I want, you refused to help me and abused me into the bargain! So now give me yours!" The poor Person of Consequence very nearly died. Resolute and determined as he was in his office and before subordinates in general, and though any one looking at his manly air and figure would have said: "Oh, what a man of charac-ter!" yet in this plight he felt, like very many persons of athletic ap-pearance, such terror that not without reason he began to be afraid he would have some sort of fit. He actually flung his overcoat off his shoulders as fast as he could and shouted to his coachman in a voice unlike his own: "Drive home and make haste!" The coachman, hearing the tone which he had only heard in critical moments and then accompanied by something even more rousing, hunched his shoulders up to his ears in case of worse following, swung his whip and flew on like an arrow. In a little over six minutes the Person of Consequence was at the entrance of his own house. Pale, panic-stricken, and without his overcoat, he arrived home instead of at Karolina Ivanovna's, dragged himself to his own room and spent the night in great perturbation, so that next morning his daughter said to him at breakfast, "You look quite pale to-day, Papa": but her papa remained mute and said not a word to anyone of what had happened to him, where he had been, and where he had been going. The incident made a great impression upon him. Indeed, it hap-pened far more rarely that he said to his subordinates, "How dare you? do you understand who I am?" and he never uttered those words at all until he had first heard all the rights of the case.

What was even more remarkable is that from that time the ap-parition of the dead clerk ceased entirely: apparently the general's overcoat had fitted him perfectly, anyway nothing more was heard of overcoats being snatched from any one. Many restless and anxious people refused, however, to be pacified, and still maintained that in remote parts of the town the ghost of the dead clerk went on appearing. One sentry in Kolomna, for instance, saw with his own eyes a ghost appear from behind a house; but, being by natural constitution somewhat feeble—so much so that on one occasion an ordinary, well-grown pig, making a sudden dash out of some building, knocked him off his feet to the vast entertainment of the cabmen standing round, from whom he exacted two kopecks each for snuff for such rudeness—he did not dare to stop it, and so followed it in the dark until the ghost suddenly looked round and, stopping, asked him: "What do you want?" displaying a fist such as you never see among the living. The sentry said: "Nothing," and turned back on the spot. This ghost, however, was considerably taller and adorned with immense moustaches, and, directing its steps apparently towards Obuhov Bridge, vanished into the darkness of the night.

# IVAN FYODOROVITCH SHPONKA

## AND HIS AUNT

HERE IS a story about this story: we were told it by Stepan Ivanovitch Kurotchka, who came over from Gadyatch. You must know that my memory is incredibly poor: you may tell me a thing or not tell it, it is all the same. It is just pouring water into a sieve. Being aware of this failing, I purposely begged him to write the story down in an exercise-book. Well, God give him good health, he was always a kind man to me, he set to work and wrote it down. I put it in the little table; I expect you know it; it stands in the corner as you come in by the door. . . . But there, I forgot that you had never been in my house. My old woman, with whom I have lived thirty years, has never learnt to read—no use hiding one's shortcomings. Well, I noticed that she baked the pies on paper of some sort. She bakes pies beautifully, dear readers; you will never taste better pies anywhere. I happened to look on the underside of a pie —what do I see? Written words! My heart seemed to tell me at once: I went to the table, only half the book was there! All the other pages she had carried off for the pies! What could I do? There is no fighting at our age! Last year I happened to be passing through

Gadyatch. Before I reached the town I purposely tied a knot in my handkerchief that I might not forget to ask Stepan Ivanovitch about it. That was not all, I vowed to myself that as soon as ever I sneezed in the town I would be sure to think of it. It was all no use. I drove through the town and sneezed and blew my nose too, but still I forgot it; and I only thought of it nearly five miles after I had passed through the town-gate. There was no help for it, I had to print it without the end. However, if any one particularly wants to know what happened later on in the story, he need only go on purpose to Gadyatch and ask Stepan Ivanovitch. He will be glad to tell the story, I daresay, all over again from the beginning. He lives not far from the brick church. There is a little lane close by, and as soon as you turn into the lane it is the second or third gate. Or better still, when you see a big post with a quail on it in the yard and coming to meet you a stout peasant woman in a green petticoat (it may be as well to mention that he is a bachelor), that is his yard. Though indeed you may meet him in the market, where he is to be seen every morning before nine o'clock, choosing fish and vegetables for his table and talking to Father Antip or the Jewish contractor. You will know him at once, for there is no one else who has trousers of flowered linen and a yellow cotton coat. And another thing you may know him by—he always swings his arms as he walks. Denis Petrovitch, the assessor, now deceased, always used to say when he saw him in the distance, "Look, look, here comes our windmill!"

## I

### IVAN FYODOROVITCH SHPONKA

It is four years since Ivan Fyodorovitch retired from the army and came to live on his farm Vytrebenki. When he was still Vanyusha, he was at the Gadyatch district school, and I must say he was a very well-behaved and industrious boy. Nikifor Timofyevitch Dyepritch-astie, the teacher of Russian grammar, used to say that if all the boys had been as anxious to do their best as Shponka, he would not have brought into the class-room the maplewood ruler with which, as he owned himself, he was tired of hitting the lazy and mischievous boys' hands. His exercise-book was always neat, with a ruled margin, and not the tiniest blot anywhere. He always sat quietly with his arms folded and his eyes fixed on the teacher, and he never used to stick scraps of paper on the back of the boy sitting in front of him, never cut the bench and never played at shoving the other boys off the bench before the master came in. If any one wanted a penknife to mend his pen, he immediately applied to Ivan Fyodorovitch know-ing that he always had a penknife, and Ivan Fyodorovitch, at that time simply Vanyusha, would take it out of a little leather case at-tached to a buttonhole of his grey coat, and would only request that the sharp edge should not be used for scraping the pen, pointing out that there was a blunt side for the purpose. Such good conduct soon attracted the attention of the Latin master, whose cough in the passage was enough to reduce the class to terror, even before his frieze coat and pockmarked countenance had appeared in the door-way.   This terrible master, who always had two birches lying on his desk and half of whose pupils were always on their knees, made Ivan Fyodorovitch monitor, although there were many boys in the class of much greater ability. Here I cannot omit an incident which had an influence on the whole of his future life. One of the boys entrusted to his charge tried to induce his monitor to write *scit* on his report, though he had not learnt his lesson, by bringing into class a pancake soaked in butter and wrapped in paper. Though Ivan Fyodorovitch was usually conscientious, on this occasion he was hungry and could not resist the temptation: he took the pancake, held a book up before him and began eating it, and he was so absorbed in this occupation that he did not observe that a deathly silence had fallen upon the class-room. He only woke up with horror when a terrible hand protruding from a frieze overcoat seized him by the ear and dragged him into the middle of the room. "Hand over that pancake! Hand it over, I tell you, you rascal!" said the terrible master; he seized the buttery pancake in his fingers and flung it out of window, sternly forbidding the boys running about in the yard to pick it up. Then he proceeded on the spot to whack Ivan Fyodorovitch very painfully on the hands; and quite rightly—the hands were responsible for taking it and no other part of the body. Anyway, the timidity which had always been characteristic of him was more marked from that time forward. Possibly the same incident was the explanation of his feeling no desire to enter the civil service, having learnt by experience that one is not always successful in hiding one's misdeeds.

He was very nearly fifteen when he moved up into the second class, where instead of the four rules of arithmetic and the abridged catechism, he went on to the longer one, the book of the duties of man, and fractions. But seeing that the further you went into the forest the thicker the wood became, and receiving the news that his father had departed this life, he stayed only two years longer at school, and with his mother's consent went in the P—— infantry regiment.

The P—— infantry regiment was not at all of the class to which many infantry regiments belong, and, although it was for the most part stationed in country places, it was in no way inferior to many cavalry regiments. The majority of the officers drank neat spirit and were quite as good at dragging about Jews by their curls as any Hussars; some of them even danced the mazurka, and the colonel of the regiment never missed an opportunity of mentioning the fact when he was talking to any one in company. "Among my officers," he used to say, patting himself on the belly after every word, "a number dance the mazurka, quite a number of them, really a great number of them indeed." To show our readers the degree of culture of the P—— infantry regiment, we must add that two of the officers were passionately fond of the game of bank and used to gamble away their uniforms, caps, overcoats, swordknots and even their underclothes, which is more than you could find in every cavalry regiment.

Contact with such comrades did not, however, diminish Ivan Fyodorovitch's timidity; and as he did not drink neat spirit, preferring to it a wineglassful of ordinary vodka before dinner and supper, did not dance the mazurka or play bank, naturally he was bound to be always left alone. And so it came to pass that while the others were driving about with hired horses, visiting the less important landowners, he sitting at home spent his time in pursuits peculiar to a mild and gentle soul: he either polished his buttons, or read a dream-book or set mouse-traps in the corners of his room, or failing everything he would take off his uniform and lie on his bed.

On the other hand, no one in the regiment was more punctual in his duties than Ivan Fyodorovitch, and he drilled his platoon in such a way that the commander of the company always held him up as a model to the others. Consequently in a short time, eleven years after becoming an ensign, he was promoted to be a second lieutenant.

During that time he had received the news that his mother was dead, and his aunt, his mother's sister, whom he only knew from her bringing him in his childhood—and even sending him when he was at Gadyatch—dried pears and extremely nice honeycakes which she made herself (she was on bad terms with his mother and so Ivan Fyodorovitch had not seen her in later years), this aunt, in the goodness of her heart, undertook to look after his little estate and in due time informed him of the fact by letter.

Ivan Fyodorovitch, having the fullest confidence in his aunt's good sense, continued to perform his duties as before. Some men in his position would have grown conceited at such promotion, but pride was a feeling of which he knew nothing, and as lieutenant he was the same Ivan Fyodorovitch as he had been when an ensign. He spent another four years in the regiment after the event of so much consequence to him, and was about to leave the Mogilyev district for Great Russia with his regiment when he received a letter as follows:

*"My Dear Nephew, Ivan Fyodorovitch,*—I am sending you some linen: five pairs of thread socks and four shirts of fine linen; and what is more I want to talk to you of something serious; since you have already a rank of some importance, as I suppose you are aware, and have reached a time of life when it is fitting to take up the management of your land, there is no reason for you to remain longer in military service. I am getting old and can no longer see to everything on your farm; and in fact there is a great deal that I want to talk to you about in person.

"Come, Vanyusha! Looking forward to the real pleasure of seeing you, I remain your very affectionate Aunt,

*"Vassilissa Tsuptchevska.*

*"P.S.*—There is a wonderful turnip in our kitchen garden, more like a potato than a turnip."

A week after receiving this letter Ivan Fyodorovitch wrote an answer as follows:

*"Honored Madam, Auntie, Vassilissa Kashparovna,*—Thank you very much for sending the linen. My socks especially are very old,

*He belonged to that class of men who do not trouble*
*their heads about trifles*

my orderly has darned them four times and that has made them very tight. As to your views in regard to my service in the army, I completely agree with you, and the day before yesterday I sent in my papers. As soon as I get my discharge I will engage a chaise. As to your commission in regard to the seed wheat and Siberian corn I cannot carry it out; there is none in all the Mogilyev province. About here pigs are mostly fed on brewers' grains together with a little beer when it has grown flat. With the greatest respect, honored madam and auntie, I remain your nephew,

*"Ivan Shponka."*

At last Ivan Fyodorovitch received his discharge with the grade of lieutenant, hired for forty roubles a Jew to drive from Mogilyev to Gadyatch, and set off in the chaise just at the time when the trees are clothed with young and still scanty leaves, the whole earth is bright with fresh green, and there is the fragrance of spring over all the fields.

## II

### THE JOURNEY

Nothing of great interest occurred on the journey. They were travelling a little over a fortnight. Ivan Fyodorovitch might have arrived a little sooner than that, but the devout Jew kept the Sabbath on the Saturdays and, putting his horse-cloth over his head, prayed the whole day. Ivan Fyodorovitch, however, as I have had occasion to mention already, was a man who did not give way to being bored. During these intervals he undid his trunk, took out his underclothes, inspected them thoroughly to see whether they were properly washed and folded; carefully removed the fluff from his new uniform, which had been made without epaulettes, and repacked it all in the best possible way. He was not fond of reading in general; and if he did sometimes look into a dream-book, it was because he liked to meet again what he had already read several times. In the same way one who lives in the town goes every day to the club, not for the sake of hearing anything new there, but in order to meet there friends with whom it has been one's habit to chat at the club from time immemorial. In the same way a government clerk will read a directory of addresses with immense satisfaction several times a day with no ulterior object, he is simply entertained by the printed list of names. "Ah! Ivan Gavrilovitch So-and-so . . ." he murmurs mutely to himself. "And here again am I! h'm . . . !" and next time he reads it over again with exactly the same exclamations.

After a fortnight's journey Ivan Fyodorovitch reached a little village some eighty miles from Gadyatch. This was on Friday. The sun had long set when with the chaise and the Jew he reached an inn.

This inn differed in no respects from other little village inns. As a rule the traveller is zealously regaled in them with hay and oats, as though he were a post-horse. But should he want to lunch as decent people do lunch, he keeps his appetite intact for some future opportunity. Ivan Fyodorovitch, knowing all this, had provided himself beforehand with two bundles of breadrings and a sausage, and asking for a glass of vodka, of which there is never a shortage in any inn, he began his supper, sitting down on a bench before an oak table which was fixed immovably in the clay floor.

Meanwhile he heard the rattle of a chaise. The gates creaked but it was a long while before the chaise drove into the yard. A loud voice was engaged in scolding the old woman who kept the inn. "I will drive in," Ivan Fyodorovitch heard, "but if I am bitten by a single bug in your inn, I will beat you, on my soul I will, you old witch! and I will give you nothing for your hay!"

A minute later the door opened and there walked in—or rather squeezed himself in—a stout man in a green frock-coat. His head rested immovably on his short neck, which seemed even thicker, from a double chin. To judge from his appearance, he belonged to that class of men who do not trouble their heads about trifles and whose whole life has passed easily.

"I wish you good day, honored sir!" he pronounced on seeing Ivan Fyodorovitch.

Ivan Fyodorovitch bowed in silence.

"Allow me to ask, to whom have I the honor of speaking?" the stout newcomer continued.

At such an examination Ivan Fyodorovitch involuntarily got up and stood at attention as he usually did when the colonel asked him a question. "Retired Lieutenant Ivan Fyodorovitch Shponka," he answered.

"And may I ask what place you are bound for?"

"My own farm Vytrebenki."

"Vytrebenki!" cried the stern examiner. "Allow me, honored sir, allow me!" he said, going towards him, and waving his arms as though some one were hindering him or as though he were making his way through a crowd, he folded Ivan Fyodorovitch in an embrace and kissed him first on the right cheek and then on the left and then on the right again. Ivan Fyodorovitch was much gratified by this kiss, for his lips were pressed against the stranger's fat cheeks as though against soft cushions.

"Allow me to make your acquaintance, my dear sir!" the fat man continued: "I am a landowner of the same district of Gadyatch and your neighbor; I live not more than four miles from your Vytrebenki in the village of Hortyshtche; and my name is Grigory Grigoryevitch Stortchenko. You really must, sir, you really must pay me a visit at Hortyshtche. I won't speak to you if you don't. I am in haste now on business. . . . Why, what's this?" he said in a mild voice to his postilion, a boy in a Cossack tunic with patched elbows and a be-wildered expression, who came in and put bags and boxes on the table. "What's this, what's the meaning of it?" and by degrees Grigory Grigoryevitch's voice grew more and more threatening. "Did I tell you to put them here, my good lad? Did I tell you to put them here, you rascal? Didn't I tell you to heat the chicken up first, you scoundrel? Be off!" he shouted, stamping. "Stay, you fright! Where's the basket with the bottles? Ivan Fyodorovitch!" he said, pouring out a glass of liqueur, "I beg you take some cordial!"

"Oh, really, I cannot . . . I have already had occasion. . . ." Ivan Fyodorovitch began hesitatingly.

"I won't hear a word, sir!" the gentleman raised his voice, "I won't hear a word! I won't budge till you drink it. . . ."

Ivan Fyodorovitch, seeing that it was impossible to refuse, not without gratification emptied the glass.

"This is a fowl, sir," said the fat Grigory Grigoryevitch, carving it in a wooden box. "I must tell you that my cook Yavdoha is fond of a drop at times and so she often dries up things. Hey, lad!" here he turned to the boy in the Cossack tunic who was bringing in a feather-bed and pillows, "make my bed on the floor in the middle of the room! Mind you put plenty of hay under the pillow! And pull a bit of hemp from the woman's distaff to stop up my ears for the night! I must tell you, sir, that I have the habit of stopping up my ears at night ever since the damnable occasion when a cockroach crawled into my left ear in a Great Russian inn. The confounded long-beards, as I found out afterwards, eat their soup with beetles in it. Impossible to describe what happened to me; there was such a tickling, such a tickling in my ear. . . . I was downright crazy! I was cured by a simple old woman in our district, and by what do you suppose? Simply by whispering to it. What do you think, my dear sir, about doctors? What I think is that they simply hoax us and make fools of us: some old women know a dozen times as much as all these doctors."

"Indeed, what you say is perfectly true, sir. There certainly are cases . . ." Here.Ivan Fyodorovitch paused as though he could not find the right word. It may not be amiss to mention here that he was at no time lavish of words. This may have been due to timidity, or it may have been due to a desire to express himself elegantly.

"Shake up the hay properly, shake it up properly!" said Grigory Grigoryevitch to his servant. "The hay is so bad about here that you may come upon a twig in it any minute. Allow me, sir, to wish you a good night! We shall not see each other to-morrow. I am setting off before dawn. Your Jew will keep the Sabbath because to-morrow is Saturday, so it is no good for you to get up early. Don't forget my invitation; I won't speak to you if you don't come to see me at Hortyshtche."

At this point Grigory Grigoryevitch's servant pulled off his coat and high boots and gave him his dressing-gown instead, and Grigory Grigoryevitch stretched on his bed, and it looked as though one huge feather-bed were lying on another.

"Hey, lad! where are you, rascal? Come here and arrange my quilt. Hey, lad, prop up my head with hay! Have you watered the horses yet? Some more hay! here, under this side! And do arrange the quilt properly, you rascal! That's right, more! Ough . . . !"

Then Grigory Grigoryevitch heaved two sighs and filled the whole room with a terrible whistling through his nose, snoring so loudly at times that the old woman who was snoozing on the settle, suddenly waking up, looked about her in all directions, but, seeing nothing, subsided and went to sleep again.

When Ivan Fyodorovitch woke up next morning, the fat gentleman was no longer there. This was the only noteworthy incident that occurred on the journey. Two days later he drew near his little farm.

He felt his heart begin to throb when the windmill waving its sails peeped out and, as the Jew drove his nag up the hill, the row of willows came into sight below. The pond gleamed bright and shining through them and a breath of freshness rose from it. Here he used to bathe in old days; in that pond he used to wade with the peasant lads, up to his neck, after crayfish. The covered cart mounted the dam and Ivan Fyodorovitch saw the little old-fashioned house thatched with reeds, and the apple trees and cherry trees which he used to climb on the sly. He had no sooner driven into the yard than dogs of all kinds, brown, black, grey, spotted, ran up from every side. Some flew under the horse's hoofs, barking, others ran behind the cart, noticing that the axle was smeared with bacon fat; one, standing near the kitchen and keeping his paw on a bone, uttered a volley of shrill barks; and another gave tongue in the distance, running to and fro wagging his tail and seeming to say: "Look, good Christians! what a fine young fellow I am!" Boys in grubby shirts ran out to stare. A sow that was promenading in the yard with sixteen little pigs lifted her snout with an inquisitive air and grunted louder than usual. In the yard a number of hempen sheets were lying on the ground covered with wheat, millet, and barley drying in the sun. A good many different kinds of herbs, such as wild chicory and swine-herb, were drying on the roof.

Ivan Fyodorovitch was so occupied in scrutinizing all this that he was only roused when a spotted dog bit the Jew on the calf of his leg as he was getting down from the box. The servants who ran out, that is, the cook and another woman and two girls in woolen petticoats, after the first exclamations: "It's our young master!" informed him that his aunt was sowing sweet corn together with the girl Palashka and Omelko the coachman, who often performed the duties of a gardener and watchman also. But his aunt, who had seen the sack-covered cart in the distance, was already on the spot. And Ivan Fyodorovitch was astonished when she almost lifted him from the ground in her arms, hardly able to believe that this could be the aunt who had written to him of her old age and infirmities.

## III

### AUNTIE

Auntie Vassilissa Kashparovna was at this time about fifty. She had never been married, and commonly declared that she valued her maiden state above everything. Though, indeed, to the best of my memory, no one ever courted her. This was due to the fact that all men were sensible of a certain timidity in her presence, and never had the spirit to make her an offer. "A girl of great character, Vassilissa Kashparovna!" all the young men used to say, and they were quite right, too, for there was no one Vassilissa Kashparovna could not get the whip hand of. With her own manly hand, tugging every day at his topknot of curls, she could, unaided, turn the drunken miller, a worthless fellow, into a perfect treasure. She was of almost gigantic stature and her breadth and strength were fully in proportion. It seemed as though nature had made an unpardonable mistake in condemning her to wear a dark brown gown with little

flounces on weekdays and a red cashmere shawl on Sunday and on her name-day, though a dragoon's moustaches and high topboots would have suited her better than anything. On the other hand, her pursuits completely corresponded with her appearance: she rowed the boat herself and was more skilful with the oars than any fisherman; shot game; stood over the mowers all the while they were at work; knew the exact number of the melons, of all kinds, in the kitchen garden; took a toll of five kopecks from every wagon that crossed her dam; climbed the trees and shook down the pears; beat lazy vassals with her terrible hand and with the same menacing hand bestowed a glass of vodka on the deserving. Almost at the same moment she was scolding, dyeing yarn, racing to the kitchen, brewing kvass, making jam with honey; she was busy all day long and everywhere in the nick of time. The result of all this was that Ivan Fyodorovitch's little property, which had consisted of eighteen souls at the last census, was flourishing in the fullest sense of the word. Moreover, she had a very warm affection for her nephew and carefully accumulated kopecks for him.

From the time of his arrival at his home Ivan Fyodorovitch's life was completely transformed and took an entirely different turn. It seemed as though nature had designed him expressly for looking after an estate of eighteen souls. Auntie herself observed that he would make an excellent farmer, though she did not yet permit him to meddle in every branch of the management. "He's but a young child yet," she used commonly to say, though Ivan Fyodorovitch was as a fact not far off forty. "How should he know it all!"

However, he was always in the fields with the reapers and mowers, and this was a source of unutterable pleasure to his gentle heart. The sweep of a dozen or more gleaming scythes in unison; the sound of the grass falling in even swathes; the carolling songs of the reapers at intervals, at one time joyous as the welcoming of a guest, at another mournful as parting; the calm pure evening—and what an evening! How free and fresh the air! How everything revived; the steppe flushed red then turned dark blue and gleamed with flowers; quails, bustards, gulls, grasshoppers, thousands of insects and all of them whistling, buzzing, churring, calling and suddenly blending into a harmonious chorus; nothing silent for an instant, while the sun sets and is hidden. Oh, how fresh and delightful it was! Here and there about the fields camp-fires are built and cauldrons set over them, and round the fires the mowers sit down; the steam from the dumplings floats upwards; the twilight turns greyer. . . . It is hard to say what passed in Ivan Fyodorovitch at such times. When he joined the mowers, he forgot to try their dumplings, though he liked them particularly, and stood motionless, watching a gull disappear in the sky or counting the sheaves of corn dotted over the field.

In a short time Ivan Fyodorovitch was spoken of as a great farmer. Auntie was never tired of rejoicing over her nephew and never lost an opportunity of boasting of him. One day—it was just after the end of the harvest, that is at the end of July—Vassilissa Kashparovna took Ivan Fyodorovitch by the arm with a mysterious air, and said she wanted now to speak to him of a matter which had long been on her mind.

"You are aware, dear Ivan Fyodorovitch," she began, "that there are eighteen souls on your farm, though, indeed, that is by the census register, and in reality they may reckon up to more, they may be twenty-four. But that is not the point. You know the copse that lies behind our vegetable ground, and no doubt you know the broad meadow behind it; there are very nearly sixty acres in it; and the grass is so good that it is worth a hundred roubles every year, especially if, as they say, a cavalry regiment is to be stationed at Gadyatch."

"To be sure, Auntie, I know: the grass is very good."

---

"You needn't tell me the grass is very good, I know it; but do you know that all that land is by rights yours? Why do you look so surprised? Listen, Ivan Fyodorovitch! You remember Stepan Kuzmitch? What am I saying: 'you remember'! You were so little that you could not even pronounce his name. Yes, indeed! How could you remember! When I came on the very eve of St. Philip's Fast and took you in my arms, you almost ruined my dress; luckily I was just in time to hand you to your nurse, Matryona; you were such a horrid little thing then . . . ! But that is not the point. All the land beyond our farm, and the village of Hortyshtche itself belonged to Stepan Kuzmitch. I must tell you that before you were in this world he used to visit your mamma—though, indeed, only when your father was not at home. Not that I say it in blame of her—God rest her soul!— though your poor mother was always unfair to me! But that is not the point. Be that as it may, Stepan Kuzmitch made a deed of gift to you of that same estate of which I have been speaking. But your poor mamma, between ourselves, was a very strange character. The devil himself (God forgive me for the nasty word!) would have been puzzled to understand her. What she did with that deed of gift— God only knows. It's my opinion that it is in the hands of that old bachelor, Grigory Grigoryevitch Stortchenko. That pot-bellied rascal has got hold of the whole estate. I'd bet anything you like that he has hidden that deed."

"Allow me to ask, Auntie: isn't he the Stortchenko whose acquaintance I made at the inn?" Hereupon Ivan Fyodorovitch described his meeting with Stortchenko.

"Who knows," said his aunt after a moment's thought, "perhaps he is not a rascal. It's true that it's only six months since he came to live among us; there's no finding out what a man is in that time. The old lady, his mother, is a very sensible woman, so I hear, and they say she is a great hand at salting cucumbers; her own serf-girls can make capital rugs. But as you say he gave you such a friendly welcome, go and see him, perhaps the old sinner will listen to his conscience and will give up what is not his. If you like you can go in the chaise, only those confounded brats have pulled out all the nails at the back; you must tell the coachman, Omelko, to nail the leather on better everywhere."

"What for, Auntie? I will take the trap that you sometimes go out shooting in."

With that the conversation ended.

## IV

### The Dinner

It was about dinner-time when Ivan Fyodorovitch drove into the hamlet of Hortyshtche and he felt a little timid as he approached the manor-house. It was a long house, not thatched with reeds like the houses of many of the neighboring landowners, but with a wooden roof. Two barns in the yard also had wooden roofs: the gate was of oak. Ivan Fyodorovitch felt like a dandy who, on arriving at a ball, sees every one more smartly dressed than himself. He stopped his trap by the barn as a sign of respect and went on foot towards the front door.

"Ah, Ivan Fyodorovitch!" cried the fat man Grigory Grigoryevitch, who was crossing the yard in his coat but without cravat, waistcoat and braces. But apparently this attire weighed oppressively on his bulky person, for the perspiration was streaming down him.

---

"Why, you said you would come as soon as you had seen your aunt, and all this time you have not been here?" After these words Ivan Fyodorovitch's lips found themselves again in contact with the same cushions.

"Chiefly being busy looking after the land. . . . I have come just for a minute to see you on business. . . ."

"For a minute? Well, that won't do. Hey, lad!" shouted the fat gentleman, and the same boy in the Cossack tunic ran out of the kitchen. "Tell Kassyan to shut the gate tight, do you hear! make it fast! And take this gentleman's horse out of the shafts this minute. Please come indoors; it is so hot out here that my shirt's soaked."

On going indoors Ivan Fyodorovitch made up his mind to lose no time and in spite of his shyness to act with decision.

"My aunt had the honor . . . she told me that a deed of gift of the late Stepan Kuzmitch . . ."

It is difficult to describe the unpleasant grimace made by the broad countenance of Grigory Grigoryevitch at these words.

"Oh dear, I hear nothing!" he responded. "I must tell you that a cockroach got into my left ear (those bearded Russians breed cockroaches in all their huts); no pen can describe what agony it was, it kept tickling and tickling. An old woman cured me by the simplest means. . . ."

"I meant to say . . ." Ivan Fyodorovitch ventured to interrupt, seeing that Grigory Grigoryevitch was intentionally changing the subject; "that in the late Stepan Kuzmitch's will mention is made, so to speak, of a deed of gift. . . . According to it I ought . . ."

"I know; so your aunt has told you that story already. It's a lie, upon my soul it is! My uncle made no deed of gift. Though, indeed, some such deed is referred to in the will. But where is it? No one has produced it. I tell you this because I sincerely wish you well. Upon my soul it is a lie!"

---

Ivan Fyodorovitch said nothing, reflecting that possibly his aunt really might be mistaken.

"Ah, here comes mother with my sisters!" said Grigory Grigoryevitch, "so dinner is ready. Let us go!"

Thereupon he drew Ivan Fyodorovitch by the hand into a room in which vodka and savories were standing on the table.

At the same time a short little old lady, a regular coffee-pot in a cap, with two young ladies, one fair and one dark, came in. Ivan Fyodorovitch, like a well-bred gentleman, went up to kiss the old lady's hand and then to kiss the hands of the two young ladies.

"This is our neighbor, Ivan Fyodorovitch Shponka, mother," said Grigory Grigoryevitch.

The old lady looked intently at Ivan Fyodorovitch, or perhaps it only seemed that she looked intently at him. She was good-natured simplicity itself, though; she looked as though she would like to ask Ivan Fyodorovitch: "How many cucumbers have you salted for the winter?"

"Have you had some vodka?" the old lady asked.

"You can't have had your sleep out, mother," said Grigory Grigoryevitch. "Who asks a visitor whether he has had anything. You offer it to him, that's all: whether we have had any or not, that is our business. Ivan Fyodorovitch! the centaury-flavored vodka or the Trofimov brand? Which do you prefer? And you, Ivan Ivanovitch, why are you standing there?" Grigory Grigoryevitch brought out, turning round, and Ivan Fyodorovitch saw the gentleman so addressed approaching the vodka, in a frock-coat with long skirts and an immense stand-up collar, which covered the whole back of his head, so that his head sat in it, as though it were a chaise.

Ivan Ivanovitch went up to the vodka and rubbed his hands, carefully examined the wineglass, filled it, held it up to the light, and poured all the vodka at once into his mouth. He did not, however, swallow it at once, but rinsed his mouth thoroughly with it first before finally swallowing it, and then after eating some bread and salted mushrooms, he turned to Ivan Fyodorovitch.

"Is it not Ivan Fyodorovitch, Mr. Shponka, I have the honor of addressing?"

"Yes, certainly," answered Ivan Fyodorovitch.

"You have changed a great deal, sir, since I saw you last. Why!" he continued, "I remember you that high!" As he spoke he held his hand a yard from the floor. "Your poor father, God grant him the kingdom of Heaven, was a rare man. He used to have melons such as you never see anywhere now. Here, for instance," he went on, drawing him aside, "they'll set melons before you on the table— such melons! You won't care to look at them! Would you believe it, sir, he used to have water-melons," he pronounced with a mysterious air, flinging out his arms as if he were about to embrace a stout tree trunk, "upon my soul as big as this!"

"Come to dinner!" said Grigory Grigoryevitch, taking Ivan Fyodorovitch by the arm.

Grigory Grigoryevitch sat down in his usual place at the end of the table, draped with an enormous tablenapkin which made him resemble the Greek heroes depicted by barbers on their signs. Ivan Fyodorovitch, blushing, sat down in the place assigned to him, facing the two young ladies; and Ivan Ivanovitch did not let slip the chance of sitting down beside him, inwardly rejoicing that he had some one to whom he could impart his various items of information.

"You shouldn't take the bishop's nose, Ivan Fyodorovitch! It's a turkey!" said the old lady, addressing Ivan Fyodorovitch, to whom the rustic waiter in a grey swallow-tail patched with black was offering a dish. "Take the back!"

---

*A short little old lady came in with two young ladies*

"Mother! no one asked you to interfere!" commented Grigory Grigoryevitch. "You may be sure our visitor knows what to take himself! Ivan Fyodorovitch! take a wing, the other one there with the gizzard! But why have you taken so little? Take a leg! Why do you stand gaping with the dish? Ask him! Go down on your knees, rascal! Say, at once, 'Ivan Fyodorovitch, take a leg!' "

"Ivan Fyodorovitch, take a leg!" the waiter with the dish bawled, kneeling down.

"H'm! do you call this a turkey?" Ivan Ivanovitch muttered in a low voice, turning to his neighbor with an air of disdain. "Is that what a turkey ought to look like? If you could see my turkeys! I assure you there is more fat on one of them than on a dozen of these. Would you believe me, sir, they are really a repulsive sight when they walk about my yard, they are so fat . . . !"

"Ivan Ivanovitch, you are telling lies!" said Grigory Grigorye-vitch, overhearing these remarks.

"I tell you," Ivan Ivanovitch went on talking to his neighbor, af-fecting not to hear what Grigory Grigoryevitch had said, "last year when I sent them to Gadyatch, they offered me fifty kopecks apiece for them, and I wouldn't take even that."

"Ivan Ivanovitch! I tell you, you are lying!" observed Grigory Grigoryevitch, dwelling on each syllable for greater distinctness and speaking more loudly than before.

But Ivan Ivanovitch behaved as though the words could not pos-sibly refer to him; he went on as before, but in a much lower voice: "Yes, sir, I would not take it. There is not a gentleman in Gad-yatch . . ."

"Ivan Ivanovitch! you are a fool, and that's the truth," Grigory Grigoryevitch said in a loud voice. "Ivan Fyodorovitch knows all about it better than you do, and doesn't believe you."

At this Ivan Ivanovitch was really offended: he said no more, but fell to putting away the turkey, even though it was not so fat as those that were a repulsive sight.

The clatter of knives, spoons and plates took the place of conversation for a time, but loudest of all was the sound made by Grigory Grigoryevitch, smacking his lips over the marrow out of the mutton bones.

"Have you," inquired Ivan Ivanovitch after an interval of silence, poking his head out of the chaise, "read the 'Travels of Korobeynikov in the Holy Land'? It's a real delight to heart and soul! Such books aren't published nowadays. I very much regret that I did not notice in what year it was written."

Ivan Fyodorovitch, hearing mention of a book, applied himself diligently to taking sauce.

"It is truly marvellous, sir, when you think that a humble artisan visited all those places: over two thousand miles, sir! over two thousand miles! Truly, it was by divine grace that it was vouchsafed him to reach Palestine and Jerusalem."

"So you say," said Ivan Fyodorovitch, who had heard a great deal about Jerusalem from his orderly, "that he visited Jerusalem."

"What are you saying, Ivan Fyodorovitch?" Grigory Grigoryevitch inquired from the end of the table.

"I had occasion to observe what distant lands there are in the world!" said Ivan Fyodorovitch, genuinely gratified that he had succeeded in uttering so long and difficult a sentence.

"Don't you believe him, Ivan Fyodorovitch!" said Grigory Grigoryevitch, who had not quite caught what he said, "he always tells fibs!"

Meanwhile dinner was over. Grigory Grigoryevitch went to his own room, as his habit was, for a little nap; and the visitors followed their aged hostess and the young ladies into the drawing-room, where the same table on which they had left vodka when they went out to dinner was now as though by some magical transformation covered with little saucers of jam of various sorts and dishes of cherries and different kinds of melons.

The absence of Grigory Grigoryevitch was perceptible in everything: the old lady became more disposed to talk and, of her own accord, without being asked, revealed several secrets in regard to the making of apple cheese, and the drying of pears. Even the young ladies began talking; though the fair one, who looked some six years younger than her sister and who was apparently about five-and-twenty, was rather silent.

But Ivan Ivanovitch was more talkative and livelier than any one. Feeling secure that no one would snub or contradict him, he talked of cucumbers and of planting potatoes and of how much more sensible people were in old days—no comparison with what people are now!—and of how as time goes on everything improves and the most intricate inventions are discovered. He was, indeed, one of those persons who take great pleasure in relieving their souls by conversation and will talk of anything that possibly can be talked about. If the conversation touched upon grave and solemn subjects, Ivan Ivanovitch sighed after each word and nodded his head slightly: if the subject were of a more homely character, he would pop his head out of his chaise and make faces from which one could almost, it seemed, read how to make pear kvass, how large were the melons of which he was speaking and how fat were the geese that were running about in his yard.

At last, with great difficulty and not before evening, Ivan Fyodorovitch succeeded in taking his leave, and although he was usually ready to give way and they almost kept him for the night by force, he persisted in his intention of going—and went.

## V

### Auntie's New Plans

"Well, did you get the deed of gift out of the old reprobate?" Such was the question with which Ivan Fyodorovitch was greeted by his aunt, who had been expecting him for some hours in the porch and had at last been unable to resist going out to the gate.

"No, Auntie," said Ivan Fyodorovitch, getting out of the trap: "Grigory Grigoryevitch has no deed of gift!"

"And you believed him? He was lying, the confounded fellow! Some day I shall come across him and I will give him a drubbing with my own hands. Oh, I'd get rid of some of his fat for him! Though perhaps we ought first to consult our court assessor and see if we couldn't get the law of him. . . . But that's not the point now. Well, was the dinner good?"

"Very . . . yes, excellent, Auntie!"

"Well, what did you have? Tell me. The old lady, I know, is a great hand at looking after the cooking."

"Curd fritters with sour cream, Auntie: a stew of stuffed pigeons . . ."

"And a turkey with pickled plums?" asked his aunt, for she was herself very skilful in the preparation of that dish.

"Yes, there was a turkey, too . . . ! Very handsome young ladies Grigory Grigoryevitch's sisters, especially the fair one!"

"Ah!" said Auntie, and she looked intently at Ivan Fyodorovitch, who dropped his eyes, blushing. A new idea flashed into her mind. "Come, tell me," she said eagerly and with curiosity, "what are her eyebrows like?" It may not be amiss to observe that Auntie considered fine eyebrows as the most important item in a woman's looks.

"Her eyebrows, Auntie, are exactly like what you described yours as being when you were young. And there are little freckles all over her face."

"Ah," commented his aunt, well pleased with Ivan Fyodorovitch's observation, though he had had no idea of paying her a compliment. "What sort of dress was she wearing? Though, indeed, it's hard to get good material nowadays, such as I have here, for instance, in this gown. But that's not the point. Well, did you talk to her about anything?"

"Talk . . . how do you mean, Auntie? Perhaps you are imagining . . ."

"Well, what of it, there would be nothing strange in that? Such is God's will! It may have been ordained at your birth that you should make a match of it."

"I don't know how you can say such a thing, Auntie. That shows that you don't know me at all. . . ."

"Well, well, now he is offended," said his aunt. "He's still only a child!" she thought to herself: "he knows nothing! We must bring them together—let them get to know each other!"

Hereupon Auntie went to have a look at the kitchen and left Ivan Fyodorovitch alone. But from that time forward she thought of nothing but seeing her nephew married as soon as possible and fondling his little ones. Her brain was absorbed in making preparations for the wedding, and it was noticeable that she bustled about more busily than ever, though the work was the worse rather than the better for it. Often when she was making the pies, a job which she never left to the cook, she would forget everything, and imagining that a tiny great-nephew was standing by her asking for some pie, would absently hold out her hands with the nicest bit for him, and the yard-dog taking advantage of this would snatch the dainty morsel and by its loud munching rouse her from her reverie, for which it was always beaten with the oven fork. She even abandoned her favorite pursuits and did not go out shooting, especially after she shot a crow by mistake for a partridge, a thing which had never happened to her before.

At last, four days later, every one saw the chaise brought out of the carriage house into the yard. The coachman Omelko (he was also the gardener and the watchman) had been hammering from early morning, nailing on the leather and continually chasing away the dogs who licked the wheels. I think it my duty to inform my readers that this was the very chaise in which Adam used to drive; and therefore, if any one gives out that some other chaise was Adam's, it is an absolute lie, and his chaise is certainly not the genuine article. It is impossible to say how it survived the Deluge. It must be supposed that there was a special coach-house for it in Noah's Ark. I am very sorry that I cannot give a living picture of it for my readers. It is enough to say that Vassilissa Kashparovna was very well satisfied with its structure and always expressed regret that the old style of carriages had gone out of fashion. The chaise had been constructed a little on one side, so that the right half stood much higher than the left, and this pleased her particularly, because, as she said, a stout person could sit on one side and a tall person on the other. Inside the chaise, however, there was room for five small persons or three such as Auntie herself.

About midday Omelko, having finished with the chaise, brought out of the stable three horses which were a little younger than the chaise, and began harnessing them with cord to the magnificent equipage. Ivan Fyodorovitch and his aunt, one on the left side and the other on the right, stepped in and the chaise drove off. The peasants they met on the road seeing this sumptuous turn-out (Vassilissa

Kashparovna rarely drove out in it) stopped respectfully, taking off their caps and bowing low.

Two hours later the chaise stopped at the front door—I think I need not say—of Stortchenko's house. Grigory Grigoryevitch was not at home. His old mother and the two young ladies came into the dining-room to receive the guests. Auntie walked in with a majestic step, with a great air stopped short with one foot in front, and said in a loud voice:

"I am delighted, dear madam, to have the honor to offer you my respects in person; and at the same time to thank you for your hospitality to my nephew, who has been warm in his praises of it. Your buckwheat is very good, madam—I saw it as we drove into the village. May I ask how many sheaves you get to the acre?"

After that followed kisses all round. As soon as they were seated in the drawing-room, the old lady began:

"About the buckwheat I cannot tell you: that's Grigory Grigoryevitch's department: it's long since I have had anything to do with the farming; indeed, I am not equal to it, I am old now! In old days I remember the buckwheat stood up to my waist; now goodness knows what it is like, though they do say everything is better now." At that point the old lady heaved a sigh, and some observers would have heard in that sigh the sigh of a past age, of the eighteenth century.

"I have heard, madam, that your own maids can make excellent carpets," said Vassilissa Kashparovna, and with that touched on the old lady's most sensitive chord: at those words she seemed to brighten up, and she talked readily of the way to dye the yarn and prepare the thread.

From carpets the conversation passed easily to the salting of cucumbers and drying of pears. In short, before the end of an hour the two ladies were talking together as though they had been friends all their lives. Vassilissa Kashparovna had already said a great deal to her in such a low voice that Ivan Fyodorovitch could not hear what she was saying.

"Yes, would not you like to have a look at them?" said the old lady, getting up.

The young ladies and Vassilissa Kashparovna also got up and all moved towards the maids' room. Auntie made a sign, however, to Ivan Fyodorovitch to remain and said something in an undertone to the old lady.

"Mashenka," said the latter, addressing the fair-haired young lady, "stay with our visitor and talk with him, that he may not be dull!"

The fair-haired young lady remained and sat down on the sofa. Ivan Fyodorovitch sat on his chair as though on thorns, blushed and cast down his eyes; but the young lady appeared not to notice this and sat unconcernedly on the sofa, carefully scrutinizing the windows and the walls, or watching the cat timorously running round under the chairs.

Ivan Fyodorovitch grew a little bolder and would have begun a conversation; but it seemed as though he had lost all his words on the way. Not a single idea came into his mind.

The silence lasted for nearly a quarter of an hour. The young lady went on sitting as before.

At last Ivan Fyodorovitch plucked up his courage. "There are a great many flies in summer, madam!" he brought out in a half-trembling voice.

"A very great many!" answered the young lady. "My brother has made a flapper out of an old slipper of mamma's on purpose to kill them, but there are lots of them still."

---

Here the conversation dropped again, and Ivan Fyodorovitch was utterly unable to find anything to say.

At last the old lady together with his aunt and the dark-haired young lady came back again. After a little more conversation, Vassilissa Kashparovna took leave of the old lady and her daughters in spite of their entreaties that they would stay the night. The three ladies came out on the steps to see their visitors off, and continued for some time nodding to the aunt and nephew, as they looked out of the chaise.

"Well, Ivan Fyodorovitch, what did you talk about when you were alone with the young lady?" Auntie asked him on the way home.

"A very discreet and well-behaved young lady, Marya Grigoryevna!" said Ivan Fyodorovitch.

"Listen, Ivan Fyodorovitch, I want to talk seriously to you. Here you are thirty-eight, thank God; you have obtained a good rank in the service—it's time to think about children! You must have a wife...."

"What, Auntie!" cried Ivan Fyodorovitch panic-stricken, "a wife! No, Auntie, for goodness' sake ... You make me quite ashamed. ... I've never had a wife.... I shouldn't know what to do with her!"

"You'll find out, Ivan Fyodorovitch, you'll find out," said his aunt, smiling, and she thought to herself: "what next, he is a perfect baby, he knows nothing!" "Yes, Ivan Fyodorovitch!" she went on aloud, "we could not find a better wife for you than Marya Grigoryevna. Besides, you are very much attracted by her. I have had a good talk with the old lady about it: she'll be delighted to see you her son-in-law. It's true that we don't know what that reprobate Grigoryevitch will say to it; but we won't consider him, and if he takes it into his head not to give her a dowry, we'll have the law of him. . . ."

At that moment the chaise drove into the yard and the ancient nags grew more lively, feeling that their stable was not far off.

"Mind, Omelko! Let the horses have a good rest first, and don't take them down to drink the minute they are unharnessed; they are overheated."

"Well, Ivan Fyodorovitch," his aunt went on as she got out of the chaise, "I advise you to think it over well. I must run to the kitchen: I forgot to tell Soloha what to get for supper, and I expect the wretched girl won't have thought of it herself."

But Ivan Fyodorovitch stood as though thunderstruck. It was true that Marya Grigoryevna was a very nice-looking young lady; but to get married . . . ! It seemed to him so strange, so peculiar, he couldn't think of it without horror. Living with a wife . . . ! Unthinkable! He would not be alone in his own room, but they would always have to be two together . . . ! Perspiration came out on his face as he sank more deeply into meditation.

He went to bed earlier than usual but in spite of all his efforts he could not go to sleep. But at last sleep, that universal comforter, came to him; but such sleep! He had never had such incoherent dreams. First, he dreamed that everything was whirling with a noise around him, and he was running and running, as fast as his legs could carry him. . . . Now he was at his last gasp. . . . All at once some one caught him by the ear. "Aïe! who is it?" "It is I, your wife!" a voice resounded loudly in his ear—and he woke up. Then he imagined that he was married, that everything in their little house was so peculiar, so strange: a double-bed stood in his room instead of a single one; his wife was sitting on a chair. He felt queer: he did not know how to approach her, what to say to her, and then he noticed that she had the face of a goose. He happened to turn aside

and saw another wife, also with the face of a goose. Turning in another direction, he saw yet a third wife; and behind him was still another. Then he was seized by panic: he dashed away into the garden: but there it was hot, he took off his hat, and—saw a wife sitting in his hat. Drops of sweat came out on his face. He put his hand in his pocket for his handkerchief and in his pocket too there was a wife; he took some cotton-wool out of his ear—and there too sat a wife. . . . Then he suddenly began hopping on one leg, and Auntie, looking at him, said with a dignified air: "Yes, you must hop on one leg now, for you are a married man." He went towards her, but his aunt was no longer an aunt but a belfry, and he felt that some one was dragging him by a rope on the belfry. "Who is it pulling me?" Ivan Fyodorovitch asked plaintively. "It is I, your wife. I am pulling you because you are a bell." "No, I am not a bell, I am Ivan Fyodorovitch," he cried. "Yes, you are a bell," said the colonel of the P— infantry regiment, who happened to be passing. Then he suddenly dreamed that his wife was not a human being at all but a sort of woolen material; that he went into a shop in Mogilyev. "What sort of stuff would you like?" asked the shopkeeper. "You had better take a wife, that is the most fashionable material! It wears well! Every one is having coats made of it now." The shopkeeper measured and cut off his wife. Ivan Fyodorovitch put her under his arm and went off to a Jewish tailor. "No," said the Jew, "that is poor material! No one has coats made of that now. . . ."

Ivan Fyodorovitch woke up in terror, not knowing where he was; he was dripping with cold perspiration.

As soon as he got up in the morning, he went at once to his fortune-teller's book, at the end of which a virtuous bookseller had in the goodness of his heart and disinterestedness inserted an abridged dream-book. But there was absolutely nothing in it that remotely resembled this incoherent dream.

Meanwhile a quite new design, of which you shall hear more in the following chapter, was being matured in Auntie's brain.

# THE

# COACH

HE SMALL TOWN of B . . . grew much
more cheerful after the . . . cavalry regiment became stationed
there. Until then it had been immeasurably boring to live in. If,
when traveling through, you glance at the small, low, plastered
houses, which stare at the street so sourly, then . . . but it is impossible to describe the feelings which rise in your heart, the intense
distress as if you had ruined yourself at cards or cracked an ill-timed
joke—in short: you do not feel well.

The clay on the houses has been crumbled away by the rain and
the walls have changed their color from white to piebald. As is cus-
tomary in our Southern towns most of the roofs are thatched with
rushes. A long time ago the Provost had ordered the small gardens
to be dispensed with for better appearance's sake. Not a single living creature is to be encountered in the streets, save perhaps a cockerel crossing the pavement rendered as soft as a pillow by the thick
dust. This the slightest rain turns to mud and then the streets of the
small town of B . . . are filled with those corpulent animals which

**153**

the local Provost calls "Frenchmen." Raising their solemn snouts from their troughs, they grunt so loudly that the traveller has no choice but to speed on his horses.

It is difficult, by the way, to meet a traveller in the small town of B . . . Occasionally, very occasionally, some landowner, who owns twelve souls, will clatter down the street in a nankeen jacket, riding in something which is a cross between a two-wheeled cart and a truck, and just visible above heaps of flour sacks as he whips a piebald mare, behind which runs a colt.

The market square itself has a somewhat sad appearance: the tailor's house juts out very foolishly, not with its whole façade, but with a corner of it. Opposite, a stone building with two windows has been in the process of being built for about fifteen years. Further away, and quite isolated, stands a modern deal fence. It is painted grey to match the color of dirt and, as an example to the other buildings, was erected by the Provost in his youth when he had not yet acquired the habit of going to sleep immediately after lunch and of taking as a nightcap a decoction dressed with dried gooseberries. Everywhere else there are only wattle hedges. In the middle of the square are the tiniest shops. In them one can always see a bundle of round cracknels, a peasant woman in a red scarf, a forty-pound block of soap, several pounds of bitter almonds, small shot for shooting, cotton material and two shop assistants perpetually playing a game of *svayka* near the doors.

But when the cavalry regiment became stationed in the district town of B . . . everything changed. The streets became variegated and enlivened—in short, assumed an entirely different character. The small low houses often saw a nimble, well-shaped officer with a plume on his head, passing by on his way to a friend to talk about crops, about the best tobacco, and sometimes to stake on a card a droshky of the type which can be called regimental. For without leaving the regiment the droshky managed to pass through everybody's hands. To-day the Major rides in it, to-morrow it appears in the Lieutenant's stables, and in a week's time you will once more see the Major's orderly greasing it with fat.

The whole of the wooden fences between the houses was littered with soldiers' caps hanging in the sun. A grey overcoat would be certain to protrude somewhere from the gates. In the side streets one came across soldiers with moustaches as hard as shoe-brushes. These moustaches were to be seen everywhere. Whenever the women gathered with baskets in the market, a moustache would be sure to look out from behind their shoulders.

The officers put new life into fashionable society, which until then comprised only the Judge, who shared a house with a deacon's wife, and the Provost, a sagacious man, but one who slept absolutely the whole day—from lunch-time to evening and from evening to lunch-time. High life became even more crowded and entertaining when the Brigadier General took up his quarters in the town. The district landowners, about whose existence, until then, nobody would have guessed, began to travel more frequently to the district town to meet the gentlemen officers and sometimes to play Banker, about which their heads held very hazy ideas, preoccupied as they were with seed sowing, errands for the wife, and rabbits.

It is a great pity that I cannot remember the circumstances in which the Brigadier General happened to give a big dinner. Tremendous preparations were made for it. The clatter of the chef's knives in the General's kitchen could be heard at the town gates. The entire market was bought up for that dinner, so that the Judge with the deacon's wife was forced to eat only buckwheat cakes and starch *kissel* jelly. The smallish yard of the General's quarters was completely filled with carts and coaches. The gathering was confined to men—officers and some of the district landowners.

The most remarkable of the landowners was Piphagor Piphagorovich Chertokutski, one of the principal gentlemen of the B . . . district, who made the greatest noise at elections and travelled to them in a dashing carriage. At one time he served in one of the cavalry regiments and belonged to the category of important and eminent officers. That is to say, he was to be seen at many balls and gatherings wherever his regiment wandered. By the way, inquiries can be made about this of the young ladies of the Tembovskaya and Simbirskaya provinces. It may very well be, that he would have acquired the same flattering reputation in other provinces too, had he not been cashiered as the result of an incident, usually termed "an unpleasant story." Whether he slapped some senior officer's face, or whether he was himself slapped, I do not remember with certainty. The main thing is, that he was asked to resign. This, by the way, caused him in no degree to lose his importance: he wore a high-waisted dress-coat like a military uniform, spurs on his high boots and, under his nose, a moustache, because without that the nobility might have thought he had served in the infantry to which he always referred with contempt. He was present at all those crowded fairs, to which the backbone of Russia—mothers, children, daughters, and fat landowners—travel for entertainment in britchkas, two-wheeled carts, tarantasses, and coaches, the like of which scarcely exist even in dreams.

He would ferret out where a cavalry regiment was to be stationed and always arrived to meet the gentlemen officers. Nimbly alighting in front of them from his small light barouche or droshky, he would speedily make their acquaintance. During the last elections he gave an excellent dinner for the nobility at which he declared that if he were only elected their marshal, he would set noblemen on the firmest footing. Generally speaking, he behaved like a nobleman, as they say in districts and provinces. He married quite a pretty girl, who brought him a dowry of two hundred souls and several thousands in cash. The cash was immediately invested in six really excellent horses, gilt locks on the doors, a tame monkey for the house, and a French majordomo. The two hundred souls with the two hundred of his own were mortgaged for some commercial speculation. In short, he was a landowner as landowners should be . . . a substantial landowner.

At the General's dinner there were, besides him, several other landowners, but there is nothing to be said about them. The remainder were military gentlemen from the same regiment and two field officers, a Colonel and a somewhat corpulent Major. The General himself was very big and stout, a good leader, by the way, according to his officers' reports. He talked in rather a thick and significant bass.

The dinner was remarkable. Sturgeon, white sturgeon, sterlet, asparagus, quails, partridges, mushrooms, all proved that the chef had not touched any alcohol for as long as twenty-four hours, and four soldiers with knives in their hands helped him, throughout the night, to make the fricassée and the jelly. An infinite number of bottles—longnecked with lafitte and shortnecked with madeira—a wonderful summer's day, windows wide open, plates of ice on the tables, dishevelled shirtfronts on the owners of spacious dress-coats, crosstalk drowned by the General's bass and watered with champagne, everything was as it should be.

After dinner all arose with a pleasant heaviness in their stomachs, and having lighted their pipes, long-stemmed and short-stemmed, left for the porch with cups of coffee in their hands.

---

"Now we might have a look at her," said the General. "Be so good, my dear fellow," he added, addressing his adjutant, quite an agile young man of pleasant appearance, "as to order the piebald mare to be brought here. You will judge for yourselves."

Here the General drew at his pipe and puffed out some smoke.

"She is not yet in very good shape. This blasted small town! There are no decent stables here. The horse"—puff, puff—"is pretty good."

"Has Your Excellency had her a long time?" said Chertokutski.

Puff, puff, puff, pu . . . puff. "Not so long. It is only about two years since I took her from the stud farm."

"And did you have the pleasure of receiving her broken in, or did you have the pleasure of breaking her in here?"

Puff, puff, pu, pu, pu . . . u . . . u . . . ff. "Here!"

Having said this, the General completely disappeared in smoke.

In the meantime a soldier leapt out from the stables. A clatter of hoofs was heard. Finally another man appeared in a white peasant's overcoat, with a huge black moustache, leading by the bridle a frightened prancing horse, which suddenly raised its head and almost lifted up the soldier, who had crouched down on the ground.

"Come on then, come on, Agrafena Ivanovna," he was saying, leading her up to the porch.

The mare's name was Agrafena Ivanovna. Strong and wild like a beautiful girl from the South, she banged with her hoofs at the wooden porch and suddenly stopped.

The General took out his pipe and began to look at Agrafena Ivanovna with complete satisfaction. The Colonel himself stepped down from the porch and took Agrafena Ivanovna by the muzzle. The Major himself tapped Agrafena Ivanovna's leg slightly. The rest clicked their tongues.

Chertokutski stepped down from the porch and approached her from behind. The soldier stood upright holding the bridle and looked straight into the eyes of the visitors, as if he wanted to jump on them.

"Very, very good," said Chertokutski. "A superb horse! And may one ask Your Excellency how it walks?"

"Her step is good, only . . . the devil knows . . . the fool of a surgeon's assistant gave her some pills and now she has been coughing for two days."

"She is very, very good! And has Your Excellency a suitable carriage to go with her?"

"A carriage? . . . But this is a riding horse."

"I know that, but I asked Your Excellency in order to find out whether you possess a carriage on a par with your horses."

"Well, I have not exactly a sufficient number of carriages. To tell you frankly, I have wanted to have a modern coach for a long time. I wrote about it to my brother, who is now in Petersburg, but do not know whether he will send it or not."

"I think, Your Excellency," remarked the Colonel, "that there is no better coach than the Viennese."

"You think rightly"—puff, puff, puff.

"Your Excellency, I possess a remarkable coach, of real Viennese workmanship."

"Which is that? The one in which you arrived?"

"Oh, no. That is an ordinary one, expressly for the purpose of driving about on my journeys, but the other . . . it is amazing, as light as a feather and when you sit down in it, then—if Your Excellency will permit me to say so—you feel just as if you were being rocked in a cradle."

"It is restful then?"

"Very, very restful. Cushions, springs, it is all as if painted on a picture."

"It sounds good."

"And how spacious it is! Indeed, your Excellency, I have never seen anything like it yet. When I was serving, ten bottles of rum and twenty pounds of tobacco could be stowed away in its boxes. In addition I always carried with me about six uniforms, underwear and two pipes, Your Excellency, the very longest kind, and you can put a whole ox into the boot."

"It sounds good."

"I paid four thousand for it, Your Excellency."

"Judging by the price it should be good. And did you buy it yourself?"

"No, Your Excellency, I obtained it by chance. It was bought by my friend, an exceptional man, a companion of my youth, whom you would have liked very much. I am on such terms with him that what is his is mine. We share everything equally. I won it from him at cards. Would Your Excellency deign to do me the honor of coming to my house for lunch to-morrow? We could look at the coach at the same time . . ."

"I do not know what to say to that. Alone, I somehow . . . unless you will allow me to bring my gentlemen officers with me?"

"I humbly request the presence of the officers. Gentlemen! I would deem it a great honor to have the pleasure of welcoming you, too, in my house."

The Colonel, the Major and the rest of the officers expressed their thanks with courteous bows.

"Your Excellency, I personally am of the opinion that if you buy a thing, then always buy a good one. If it is mediocre, it is not worth acquiring. When you do me the honor of calling at my place to-morrow, I shall show you some of the things I have myself introduced into my household."

The General looked up and puffed out some smoke from his mouth.

Chertokutski was very pleased that he had invited the officers to his place. In his mind he was already ordering pies and sauces in anticipation, and from time to time he looked gayly at the gentlemen officers, who, for their part, somehow redoubled towards him their benevolence, which was apparent in their eyes and in the slight movements of their bodies in the shape of semi-bows. Chertokutski stalked about somehow more freely and his voice assumed weakness —the tone of a voice burdened by satisfaction.

"There you will make the acquaintance of the lady of the house, Your Excellency."

"It will give me great pleasure," said the General, stroking his moustache.

After this, Chertokutski wanted to go home immediately in order to prepare everything for the reception of his guests on the following day. He had already taken his hat in his hands, when somehow it unaccountably so happened that he lingered on. In the meantime card tables were set out in the room. Soon the whole gathering, divided into parties of four for whist, was placed in various corners of the General's room.

Candles were brought in. For a long time Chertokutski did not know whether he should or should not sit down to play whist. But when the gentleman officers began to invite him, it seemed to him completely incompatible with the rules of sociable behavior to refuse—and he sat down just for a moment. A glass of punch suddenly appeared before him and, without thinking, he drank it. Having played two rubbers, Chertokutski again found a glass of punch within his reach, and again, without thinking, drank it, saying first, "Gentlemen, it is time for me to go home. It really is."

But again he sat down for a short time to play another game. In the meantime the conversation in various corners of the room assumed an entirely private character. Those playing whist were comparatively taciturn, but those who were not playing and were sitting aside on couches, held a conversation of their own.

In one corner the second captain of cavalry, having put a cushion under his side and with a pipe in his teeth, was discussing his love affairs quite freely and fluently and completely monopolized the attention of the circle which had gathered around him. One extremely fat landowner with short hands, somewhat resembling two overgrown potatoes, listened with an unusually sweet expression, only striving from time to time to put his short little hand behind his broad back to pull out his snuffbox.

In another corner quite a heated argument ensued about squadron instruction, and Chertokutski, who had already played a Queen twice instead of a Jack, would suddenly interpose in their discussion, and shout from his corner: "In what year?" or "Of which regiment?" without noticing that sometimes the questions were entirely irrelevant.

At last, several minutes before dinnertime, the whist stopped, but it still continued in words, and it seemed that all heads were filled with whist. Chertokutski remembered very well that he had won a lot, but did not recall taking any tricks. Getting up from the table, he stood for a long time in the posture of a man who has no handkerchief in his pocket.

Meanwhile dinner was served. Naturally, there was no lack of wine, and Chertokutski, almost involuntarily, had to fill his glass from time to time, as bottles stood to the right and left of him.

Conversation was protracted at the table, but, by the way, it was somewhat strangely conducted. One Colonel, who had served in the campaign of 1812, told of some battle which had never taken place, and afterwards, for some quite obscure reason, took the stopper out of a carafe and stuck it into a pastry. In short, it was already three o'clock when they began to disperse and the drivers had to carry out several persons bodily, as if they were parcels of merchandise. And Chertokutski, in spite of all his nobility, bowed so deeply sitting in the coach and with such a waving of his head that, when he arrived home, he brought back in his moustache two buds of burdock.

The whole house was asleep. The driver, after some difficulty, managed to find the valet de chambre who led his master through the lounge and turned him over to the chamber-maid. Following her, Chertokutski somehow reached the bedroom and dropped down near his pretty young wife, who lay delightfully asleep in a nightdress as white as snow.

The motion caused by the fall of her husband on the bed awakened her. Stretching herself, she raised her eyelashes and, quickly screwing up her eyes three times, she opened them with a half angry smile. But seeing that this time he decidedly did not want to impart any caress, she turned on the other side with annoyance. Putting her fresh little cheek on her hand she soon fell asleep again.

The time of day had already arrived which in villages is not called early, when the young house-wife awoke beside her snoring husband. Remembering that he had returned home at about four o'clock in the morning, she felt loath to wake him, and, putting on her bedroom slippers, which her husband had ordered from Petersburg, and a white blouse, which draped itself around her like flowing water, she left for her dressing room. She washed with water as

*She lay delightfully asleep in a nightdress white as snow*

fresh as herself and approached her dressing table. She glanced at herself once or twice and saw that she did not look at all bad. This apparently insignificant conclusion compelled her to sit before the mirror for exactly two extra hours. At last she dressed very pleasantly and left for the garden to refresh herself.

As if by design the weather was wonderful, such as only a Southern summer's day can boast. The sun, which had come out at noon, scorched with all the power of its rays. But in the dark, thickly planted alleys it was quite cool to walk and the flowers, warmed by the sun, trebled their perfume. The pretty hostess completely forgot that it was already twelve o'clock and that her husband was still asleep. The snores of two cabdrivers and one postillion, who were sleeping in the stables behind the garden, reached her ears. But she continued to sit in the dark alley from which there opened a wide view of the road, and absent-mindedly gazed at its emptiness, when suddenly dust, which appeared from afar, attracted her attention. Looking more closely, she soon saw several carriages.

In front drove an open two-seater, in which sat the General with his fat epaulettes which glittered in the sun, and next to him sat the Colonel. It was followed by a four-seater. In this sat the Major with the General's Adjutant and two other officers who sat opposite them. Behind that coach followed the droshky, known to the whole regiment, in which this time sat the corpulent Major. Behind the droshky drove a four-seater carriage, in which sat four officers, with a fifth sprawled across their knees. Behind this carriage three officers could be seen displaying themselves on magnificent dappled and piebald horses.

"Are they really coming to us?" thought Chertokutski's wife. "Ach, Heavens! They are! They have turned on to the bridge."

She screamed, clasped her hands and ran over flower-beds and flowers straight into her husband's bedroom. He slept the sleep of the just.

"Get up! Get up! Hurry and get up!" she shouted, pulling at his hand.

"Eh?" uttered Chertokutski, and stretched himself without opening his eyes.

"Get up, darling! Can't you hear? Guests!"

"Guests? What guests?"

Having said this, he emitted a short braying, like a calf searching with its muzzle for its mother's teats.

"M'm . . ." he mumbled. "Stretch out your little neck, Cookums! Let me kiss you."

"Sweetheart, get up, for Heaven's sake, hurry! The General with the officers! Ach, my God, there is burdock in your moustache."

"The General? Is he coming already? And why the devil has nobody wakened me up? And lunch, what about lunch? Is everything prepared as it should be?"

"What lunch?"

"Didn't I tell you?"

"Tell me? You came back at four this morning and however much I asked you, you told me nothing. Therefore, Snookums, I did not wake you. I was sorry for you. You hadn't slept at all . . ."

The last words she said in an extremely languishing and imploring voice.

Chertokutski's eyes protruded. For a minute he lay in bed as if thunderstruck. At last he jumped out, dressed only in his shirt, forgetting that it was not altogether decent.

"Ach, what a horse I am!" he said, hitting himself on the forehead. "I asked them to lunch! What is there to be done? Are they far away?"

"I don't know . . . they should be here any minute."

"Sweetheart . . . hide! Hey, who's there? You, girl! Come here, you fool. What are you afraid of? Officers will arrive any minute. Say the master is not at home. Say that he will not be back at all, that he left early in the morning . . . D'you hear? And tell it to all the servants. Go on, hurry!"

Having said this, he hurriedly grabbed his dressing gown and ran to hide in the coach barn, assuming that there he would be quite free from danger. But, standing in the corner of the barn, he realized that even here he might somehow be spotted.

"Ah, this will be better!" flashed through his mind, and in a second he threw down the steps of a coach which stood near, jumped up and closed the door behind him. For greater safety he covered himself with the leather cover and remained absolutely quiet, doubled up in his dressing gown.

In the meantime the coaches drew up to the house.

The General alighted and shook himself. After him came the Colonel, attending with his hands to the plume on his hat. Then the fat Major jumped from the droshky, holding his sabre under his arm. Then from the four-seater leaped the thin Second Lieutenants and the Ensign who had been ensconced between them and finally the officers who had been displaying themselves on their horses alighted from their mounts.

"The master's not at home," said the lackey coming out on to the porch.

"What do you mean—not at home? Anyhow, he must be back here for lunch."

"Sorry, sir, he won't be. They drove away for the whole day. They might be back, perhaps, to-morrow at this time."

"This is a nuisance!" said the General. "What can have happened?"

"I admit it is awkward," said the Colonel laughing.

---

**167**

"But really, how can people act like this?" continued the General with displeasure. "What the devil . . . After all, if you cannot receive people, why force your hospitality on them?"

"Your Excellency, I cannot understand how any one could do that," said one young officer.

"What?" said the General, who was always in the habit of using this interrogative pronoun when talking to a subaltern.

"I was saying, Your Excellency, how can one act in such a manner?"

"Naturally . . . if anything has gone wrong—at least let one know or do not issue an invitation."

"Your Excellency, there is nothing to be done now. Let us go back," said the Colonel.

"Naturally, there is no other course. By the way, we can have a look at the coach without him. He has probably not taken it with him. Hey, you there! Come here, man!"

"What is it you wish, sir?"

"Are you a groom?"

"I am, Your Excellency."

"Show us the new coach, which your master obtained recently."

"Yes, Sir. Would you come into the barn?"

The General and the officers went into the barn.

"If you'll wait, I'll wheel it out a little, it's a bit dark in here."

"Very good, very good! That will do."                  .

"Well, there is nothing extraordinary about it," said the General, "the coach is quite commonplace."

"It seems to me, Your Excellency, it is not worth four thousand at all," said one of the young officers.

"What?"

"I was saying, Your Excellency, that it seems to me it is not worth four thousand."

"Never mind four thousand. It is not worth two. There is simply nothing in it. Unless there is something special inside . . . Be so good, dear fellow, as to unbutton the cover . . ."

And Chertokutski appeared before the officers' eyes, sitting doubled up in an extraordinary way in his dressing gown.

"Ah, you are here . . ." said the amazed General.

Having said this, the General instantly slammed the door, covered Chertokuski again, and drove away with the gentlemen officers.

# A MADMAN'S

# DIARY

T O-DAY an extraordinary event occurred. I got up rather late in the morning, and when Mavra brought me my cleaned boots I asked her the time. Hearing that it was long past ten I made haste to dress. I own I wouldn't have gone to the department at all, knowing the sour face the chief of our section will make me. For a long time past he has been saying to me: "How is it, my man, your head always seems in a muddle? Sometimes you rush about as though you were crazy and do your work so that the devil himself could not make head or tail of it, you write the title with a small letter, and you don't put in the date or the number." The damned heron! To be sure, he is jealous because I sit in the director's room and mend pens for his Excellency. In short I wouldn't have gone to the department if I had not hoped to see the counting-house clerk and to find out whether maybe I could not get something of my month's salary in advance out of that wretched Jew. That's another creature! Do you suppose he would ever let one have a month's pay in advance? Good gracious! the heavens would fall before he'd do

---

it! You may ask till you burst, you may be at your last farthing, but the grey-headed devil won't let you have it—and when he is at home his own cook slaps him in the face; everybody knows it. I can't see the advantage of serving in a department; there are absolutely no possibilities in it. In the provincial government, or in the civil and crown offices, it's quite a different matter: there you may see some wretched man squeezed into the corner, copying away, with a nasty old coat on and such a face that it nearly makes you sick, but look what a villa he takes! It's no use offering him a gilt china cup: "That's a doctor's present," he will say. You must give him a pair of trotting horses or a droshky or a beaver fur worth three hundred roubles. He is such a quiet fellow to look at, and says in such a refined way: "Oblige me with a pen-knife just to mend a pen," but he fleeces the petitioners so that he scarcely leaves them a shirt to their backs. It is true that ours is a gentlemanly office, there is a cleanliness in everything such as is never seen in provincial offices, the tables are mahogany and all the heads address you formally. . . . I must confess that if it were not for the gentlemanliness of the service I should have left the department long ago.

I put on my old greatcoat and took my umbrella, as it was raining in torrents. There was no one in the streets; some women pulling their skirts up to cover themselves, and some Russian merchants under umbrellas and some messengers met my eye. I saw none of the better class except one of ourselves. I saw him at the cross-roads. As soon as I saw him I said to myself: "No, my dear man, you are not on your way to the department; you are running after that girl who is racing ahead and looking at her feet." What sad dogs clerks are! Upon my soul, they are as bad as any officer: if any female goes by in a hat they are bound to be after her. While I was making this reflection I saw a carriage driving up to the shop which I was passing. I recognized it at once. It was our director's carriage. "But he can have nothing to go to the shop for," I thought; "I suppose it must be his daughter." I flattened myself against the wall. The footman opened the carriage door and she darted out like a bird. How she glanced from right to left, how her eyes and eyebrows gleamed. . . . Good God, I am done for, done for utterly! And why does she drive out in such rain! Don't tell me that women have not a passion for all this frippery. She didn't know me, and, indeed, I tried to muffle myself up all I could, because I had on a very muddy greatcoat of an old-fashioned cut. Now people wear cloaks with long collars while I had short collars one above the other, and, indeed, the cloth was not at all rainproof. Her little dog, who had been too late to dash in at the door, was left in the street. I know the dog—her name is Madgie. I had hardly been there a minute when I heard a thin little voice: "Good morning, Madgie." "Well, upon my soul! Who's that speaking?" I looked round me and saw two ladies walking along under an umbrella: one old and the other young; but they had passed already and again I heard beside me: "It's too bad of you, Madgie!" What the devil! I saw that Madgie was sniffing at a dog that was following the ladies. "Aha," I said to myself, "but come, surely I am drunk! Only I fancy that very rarely happens to me." "No, Fido, you are wrong there," said Madgie—I saw her say it with my own eyes. "I have been, wow, wow, I have been very ill, wow, wow, wow!" "Oh, so it's you, you little dog! Goodness me!" I must own I was very much surprised to hear her speaking like a human being; but afterwards, when I thought it all over, I was no longer surprised. A number of similar instances have as a fact occurred. They say that in England a fish popped up and uttered two words in such a strange language that the learned men have been for three years trying to interpret them and have not succeeded yet.

I have read in the papers of two cows also who went into a shop and asked for a pound of tea. But I must own I was much more surprised when Madgie said: "I did write to you, Fido; I expect Polkan did not take my letter." Dash it all! I never in all my life heard of a dog being able to write. No one but a gentleman born can write correctly. It's true, of course, that some shopmen and even serfs can sometimes write a little; but their writing is for the most part mechanical: they have no commas, no stops, no style.

It amazed me. I must confess that of late I have begun seeing and hearing things such as no one has ever seen or heard before. "I'll follow that dog," I said to myself, "and find out what she is like and what she thinks." I opened my umbrella and set off after the two ladies. They passed into Gorohovy Street, turned into Myestchansky and from there into Stolyarny Street; at last they reached Kokushin Bridge and stopped in front of a big house. "I know that house," I said to myself. "That's Zvyerkov's Buildings. What a huge edifice! All sorts of people live in it: such lots of cooks, of visitors from all parts! and our friends the clerks, one on the top of another, with a third trying to squeeze in, like dogs. I have a friend living there, who plays capitally on the horn." The ladies went up to the fifth storey. "Good," I thought, "I won't go in now, but I will note the place and I will certainly take advantage of the first opportunity."

*October* 4.

Today is Wednesday, and so I was in our chief's study. I came a little early on purpose and, sitting down, began mending the pens. Our director must be a very clever man. His whole study is lined with bookshelves. I have read the titles of some of them: they are all

*I flattened myself against the wall, and she darted out like a bird*

learned, so learned that they are quite beyond any one like me—
they are all either in French or in German. And just look into his
face! Ough! what importance in his eyes! I have never heard him say
a word too much. Only sometimes when one hands him the papers
he'll ask: "What's it like out of doors?" "Damp, your Excellency."
Yes, he is a cut above any one like me! He's a statesman. I notice,
however, he is particularly fond of me. If his daughter, too, were
. . . Ah, you rascal! . . . Never mind, never mind, silence! I read
*The Bee*. They are stupid people, the French! What do they want?
I'd take the lot of them, upon my word I would, and thrash them all
soundly! In it I read a very pleasant description of a ball written by
a country gentleman of Kursk. The country gentlemen of Kursk
write well. Then I noticed it was half-past twelve and that our chief
had not come out of his bedroom. But about half-past one an event
occurred which no pen could describe. The door opened, I thought
it was the director and jumped up from my chair with my papers,
but it was she, she herself! Holy saints, how she was dressed! Her
dress was white as a swan—ough, how sumptuous! And the look in
her eye—like sunshine, upon my soul, like sunshine. She bowed and
said: "Hasn't Papa been here?" Aie, aie, aie, what a voice! A canary, a regular canary. "Your Excellency," I was on the point of
saying, "do not bid them punish me, but if you want to punish, then
punish with your own illustrious hand." But dash it all, my tongue
would not obey me, and all I said was: "No, madam." She looked
at me, looked at the books, and dropped her handkerchief. I dashed
forward, slipped on the damned parquet and almost smashed my
nose but recovered myself and picked up the handkerchief. Saints,
what a handkerchief! The most delicate batiste—amber, perfect amber! you would know from the very scent that it belonged to a general's daughter. She thanked me and gave a faint smile, so that her

sugary lips scarcely moved, and after that went away. I stayed on another hour, when the footman came in and said: "You can go home, Aksenty Ivanovitch, the master has gone out." I cannot endure the flunkey set: they are always lolling about in the vestibule and don't as much as trouble themselves to nod. That's nothing: once one of the beasts had the effrontery to offer me his snuff-box without even getting up from his seat. Doesn't the fellow know I am a government clerk, that I am a gentleman by birth! However, I took my hat and put on my greatcoat myself, for these gentry never help me on with it, and went off. At home I spent most of the time lying on my bed. Then I copied out some very good verses:

> "My love for one hour I did not see,
> And a whole year it seemed to me.
>
> How life is now a hated task,
> How can I live this life, I ask."

It must have been written by Pushkin. In the evening, wrapping myself up in my greatcoat, I went to the front door of her Excellency's house and waited about for a long time on the chance of her coming out to get into her carriage, that I might snatch another glimpse of her.

*November* 6.

The head of our section was in a fury to-day. When I came into the department he called me into his room and began like this: "Come, kindly tell me what you are doing?" "How do you mean?" I said. "I am doing nothing." "Come, think what you are about!

---

178

Why, you are over forty. It's time you had a little sense. What do you imagine yourself to be? Do you suppose I don't know all the tricks you are up to? Why, you are dangling after the director's daughter! Come, look at yourself; just think what you are! Why, you are a nonentity and nothing else! Why, you haven't a penny to bless yourself with. And just look at yourself in the looking-glass—how could you think of such a thing!" Dash it all, because his face is rather like a medicine bottle and he has a shock of hair on his head curled in a tuft, and pomades it into a kind of rosette, and holds his head in the air, he imagines he is the only one who may do anything. I understand, I understand why he is in such a rage with me. He is envious: he has seen perhaps signs of preference shown to me. But I spit on him! As though a court councillor were of so much consequence! He hangs a gold chain on his watch and orders boots at thirty roubles—but deuce take him! Am I some plebeian—a tailor or a son of a non-commissioned officer? I am a gentleman. Why, I may rise in the service too. I am only forty-two, a time of life in which a career in the service is really only just beginning. Wait a bit, my friend! we too shall be a colonel and perhaps, please God, something better. We shall set up a flat, and better maybe than yours. A queer notion you have got into your head that no one is a gentleman but yourself. Give me a fashionably cut coat and let me put on a cravat like yours—and then you wouldn't hold a candle to me. I haven't the means, that's the trouble.

*November* 8.

I have been to the theatre. It was a performance of the Russian fool Filatka. I laughed very much. There was a vaudeville too, with some amusing verses about lawyers, and especially about a collegiate registrar, very freely written so that I wondered that the censor had passed it; and about the merchants they openly said that they cheat the people and that their sons are debauched and ape the gentry. There was a very amusing couplet about the journalists too: saying that they abused every one and that an author begged the public to defend him against them. The authors do write amusing plays nowadays. I love being at the theatre. As soon as I have a coin in my pocket I can't resist going. And among our dear friends the officials there are such pigs; they positively won't go to the theatre, the louts; unless perhaps you give them a free ticket. One actress sang very nicely. I thought of her . . . ah, you rascal! . . . Never mind, never mind . . . silence!

*November* 9.

At eight o'clock I went to the department. The head of our section put on a look as though he did not see me come in. On my side, too, I behaved as though nothing had passed between us. I looked through and checked some papers. I went out at four o'clock. I walked by the director's house, but no one was to be seen. After dinner for the most part lay on my bed.

*November* 11.

To-day I sat in our director's study. I mended 23 pens for him and for her . . . aie, aie! for her Excellency 4 pens. He likes to have a lot of pens. Oo, he must have a head! He always sits silent, and I expect he is turning over everything in his head. I should like to know what he thinks most about. What is going on in that head? I should like to get a close view of the life of these gentlemen, of all these *équivoques* and court ways. How they go on and what they do in their circle—that's what I should like to find out! I have several times thought of beginning a conversation on the subject with his Excellency, but, dash it all! I couldn't bring my tongue to it; one says it's cold or warm to-day and can't utter another word. I should like to look into the drawing-room, of which one only sees the open door and another room beyond it. Ah, what sumptuous furniture! What mirrors and china! I long to have a look in there, into the part of the house where her Excellency is, that's where I should like to go! Into her boudoir where there are all sorts of little jars, little bottles, and such flowers that one is frightened even to breathe on them, to see her dresses lying scattered about, more like ethereal gossamer than dresses. I long to glance into her bedroom, there I fancy there must be marvels . . . a paradise, such as is not to be found in the heavens. To look at the little stool on which she puts her little foot when she gets out of bed and the way she puts a stocking on that little snow-white foot. . . . Aie, aie, aie! never mind, never mind . . . silence.

But to-day a light as it were dawned upon me. I remembered the conversation between the two dogs that I heard on the Nevsky Prospect. "Good," I thought to myself, "now I will learn all. I must get hold of the correspondence that these wretched dogs have been carrying on. Then I shall certainly learn something." I must own I once called Madgie to me and said to her: "Listen, Madgie; here we are alone. If you like I will shut the door too, so that no one shall see you; tell me all you know about your young lady: what she is like and how she behaves. I swear I won't tell any one." But the sly little dog put her tail between her legs, doubled herself up and went quickly to the door as though she hadn't heard. I have long suspected that dogs are far more intelligent than men; I am even convinced that they can speak, only there is a certain doggedness about them. They are extremely diplomatic: they notice everything, every step a man takes. Yes, whatever happens I will go tomorrow to Zvyerkov's Buildings, I will question Fido, and if I am successful I will seize all the letters Madgie has written her.

*November* 12.

At two o'clock in the afternoon I set out determined to see Fido and question her. I can't endure cabbage, the smell of which floats from all the little shops in Myestchansky Street; moreover, such a hellish reek rises from under every gate that I raced along at full speed holding my nose. And the nasty workmen let off such a lot of soot and smoke from their workshops that a gentleman cannot walk there. When I climbed up to the sixth storey and rang the bell, a girl who was not at all bad-looking, with little freckles, came to the door. I recognized her: it was the girl who was with the old lady. She turned a little red, and I said to myself at once: "You are on the lookout for a young man, my dear." "What do you want?" she asked. "I want to have a few words with your dog." The girl was silly. I saw at once that she was silly. At that moment the dog ran out barking; I tried to catch hold of her, but the nasty wretch almost snapped at my nose. However, I saw her bed in the corner. Ah, that was just what I wanted. I went up to it, rummaged in the straw in the wooden box, and to my indescribable delight pulled out a packet of little slips of paper. The wretched dog, seeing this, first bit my calf, and then when she perceived that I had taken her letters

---

began to whine and fawn on me, but I said: "No, my dear, good-bye." and took to my heels. I believe the girl thought I was a madman, as she was very much frightened. When I got home I wanted to set to work at once to decipher the letters, for I don't see very well by candlelight; but Mavra had taken it into her head to wash the floor. These stupid Finnish women always clean at the wrong moment. And so I went out to walk about and think over the incident. Now I shall find out all their doings and ways of thinking, all the hidden springs, and shall get to the bottom of it all. These letters will reveal everything. Dogs are clever creatures, they understand all the diplomatic relations, and so no doubt I shall find there everything about our gentleman: the portrait and all the doings of the man. There will be something in them too about her who . . . never mind, silence! Towards evening I came home. For the most part I lay on my bed.

*November* 13.

Well, we shall see! The writing is fairly distinct, at the same time there is something doggy about the hand. Let us read:

"*Dear Fido,*—I never can get used to your plebeian name. As though they could not have given you a better one? Fido, Rose—what vulgarity! No more about that, however. I am very glad we thought of writing to each other."

The letter is very well written. The punctuation and even the spelling is quite correct. Even the chief of our section could not write like this, though he does talk of having studied at some university. Let us see what comes next.

"It seems to me that to share one's ideas, one's feelings, and one's impressions with others is one of the greatest blessings on earth."

---

**183**

H'm! . . . an idea taken from a work translated from the German. I don't remember the name of it.

"I say this from experience, though I have not been about the world, beyond the gates of our house. Is not my life spent in comfort? My young lady, whom her papa calls Sophie, loves me passionately."

Aie, aie! never mind, never mind! Silence!

"Papa, too, often caresses me. I drink tea and coffee with cream. Ah, *ma chère,* I ought to tell you that I see nothing agreeable at all in big, gnawed bones such as our Polkan crunches in the kitchen. The only bones that are nice are those of game, and then only when the marrow hasn't been sucked out of them by some one. What is very good is several sauces mixed together, only they must be free from capers and green stuff; but I know nothing worse than giving dogs little balls of bread. A gentleman sitting at the table who has been touching all sorts of nasty things with his hands begins with those hands rolling up bread, calls one up and thrusts the ball upon one. To refuse seems somehow discourteous—well, one eats it—with repulsion, but one eats it. . . ."

What the devil's this! What nonsense! As though there were nothing better to write about. Let us look at another page and see if there is nothing more sensible.

"I shall be delighted to let you know about everything that happens here. I have already told you something about the chief gentleman, whom Sophie calls papa. He is a very strange man."

Ah, here we are at last! Yes, I knew it; they have a very diplomatic view of everything. Let us see what Papa is like.

". . . a very strange man. For the most part he says nothing; he very rarely speaks. But about a week ago he was continually talking to himself: 'Shall I receive it or shall I not?' He would take a paper in one hand and close the other hand empty and say:

'Shall I receive it or shall I not?' Once he turned to me with the question: 'What do you think, Madgie, shall I receive it or not?' I couldn't understand a word of it, I sniffed at his boots and walked away. A week later, *ma chère,* he came in in high glee. All the morning gentlemen in uniform were coming to see him and congratulating him on something. At table he was merrier than I have ever seen him; he kept telling stories. And after dinner he lifted me up to his neck and said: 'Look, Madgie, what's this?' I saw a little ribbon. I sniffed it, but could discover no aroma whatever; at last I licked it on the sly: it was a little bit salt."

H'm! This dog seems to me to be really too . . . she ought to be thrashed! And so he is ambitious! One must take that into consideration.

"Farewell, *ma chère!* I fly, and so on . . . and so on . . . I will finish my letter to-morrow. Well, good-day, I am with you again. To-day my young lady Sophie . . ."

Oh come, let us see about Sophie. Ah, you rascal. . . . Never mind, never mind . . . let us go on.

"My young lady Sophie was in a great fluster. She was getting ready to go to a ball, and I was delighted that in her absence I could write to you. My Sophie is always very glad to go to a ball, though she always gets almost angry when she is being dressed. I cannot understand why people dress. Why don't they go about as we do, for instance? It's nice and it's comfortable. I can't understand, *ma chère,* what pleasure there is in going to balls. Sophie always comes home from balls at six o'clock in the morning, and I can almost always guess from her pale and exhausted face that they had given the poor thing nothing to eat. I must own I couldn't live like that. If I didn't get grouse and gravy or the roast wing of a chicken, I don't know what would become of me. Gravy is nice too with grain in it, but with carrots, turnips, or artichokes it is never good."

Extraordinary inequality of style! You can see at once that it is not a man writing; it begins as it ought and ends with dogginess. Let us look at one more letter. It's rather long. H'm! and there's no date on it.

"Ah, my dear, how one feels the approach of spring! My heart beats as though I were always expecting some one. There is always a noise in my ears so that I often stand for some minutes with my foot in the air listening at doors. I must confide to you that I have a number of suitors. I often sit at the window and look at them. Oh, if only you knew what ugly creatures there are among them. One is a very ungainly yard-dog, fearfully stupid, stupidity is painted on his face; he walks about the street with an air of importance and imagines that he is a distinguished person and thinks that everybody is looking at him. Not a bit of it. I don't take any notice of him—I behave exactly as though I didn't see him. And what a terrible Great Dane stops before my window! If he were to stand upon his hind legs, which I expect the clumsy fellow could not do, he would be a whole head taller than my Sophie's papa, though he is fairly tall and stout. That blockhead must be a frightfully insolent fellow. I growled at him, but much he cared: he hardly frowned, he put out his tongue, dangled his huge ears and looked up at the window—such a country bumpkin! But can you suppose, *ma chère,* that my heart makes no response to any overture? Ah no. . . . If only you could see one of my suitors climbing over the fence next door, by name Tresor. . . . Ah, *ma chère,* what a face he has! . . ."

Ough, the devil! . . . What rubbish! How can any one fill a letter with foolishness! Give me a man! I want to see a man. I want spiritual sustenance—in which my soul might find food and enjoyment; and instead of that I have this nonsense. . . . Let us turn over the page and see whether it is better!

"Sophie was sitting at the table sewing something, I was looking out of window because I am fond of watching passers-by, when all at once the footman came in and said 'Teplov!' 'Ask him in,' cried Sophie, and rushed to embrace me. 'Ah Madgie, Madgie! If only you knew who that is: a dark young man, a kammer-junker, and such eyes, black as agates!' And Sophie ran off to her room. A minute later a kammer-junker with black whiskers came in, walked up to the looking-glass, smoothed his hair and looked about the room. I growled and sat in my place. Sophie soon came in and bowed gaily in response to his scraping; and I just went on looking out of the window as though I were noticing nothing. However, I bent my head a little on one side and tried to hear what they were saying. Oh, *ma chère,* the nonsense they talked! They talked about a lady who had mistaken one figure for another at the dance; and said that some one called Bobov with a ruffle on his shirt looked just like a stork and had almost fallen down on the floor, and that a girl called Lidin imagined that her eyes were blue when they were really green —and that sort of thing. 'Well,' I thought to myself, 'if one were to compare that kammer-junker to Tresor, heavens, what a difference!' In the first place, the kammer-junker has a perfectly flat face with whiskers all round as though he had tied it up in a black handkerchief; while Tresor has a delicate little countenance with a white patch on the forehead. It's impossible to compare the kammer-junker's figure with Tresor's. And his eyes, his ways, his manners are all quite different. Oh, what a difference! I don't know, *ma chère,* what she sees in her Teplov. Why she is so enthusiastic about him. . . ."

Well, I think myself that there is something wrong about it. It's impossible that she can be fascinated by Teplov. Let us see what next.

---

"It seems to me that if she is attracted by that kammer-junker she will soon be attracted by that clerk that sits in papa's study. Oh, *ma chère*, if you knew what an ugly fellow that is! A regular tortoise in a bag. . . ."

What clerk is this? . . .

"He has a very queer surname. He always sits mending the pens. The hair on his head is very much like hay. Papa sometimes sends him out instead of a servant. . . ."

I do believe the nasty little dog is alluding to me. But my hair isn't like hay!

"Sophie can never help laughing when she sees him."

That's a lie, you damned little dog! What an evil tongue! As though I didn't know that that is the work of envy! As though I didn't know whose tricks were at the bottom of that! This is all the doing of the chief of my section. The man has vowed eternal hatred, and here he tries to injure me again and again, at every turn. Let us look at one more letter though. Perhaps the thing will explain itself.

*"My Dear Fido,*—Forgive me for not writing for so long. I have been in a perfect delirium. How truly has some writer said that love is a second life. Moreover, there are great changes in the house here. The kammer-junker is here every day. Sophie is frantically in love with him. Papa is very good-humored. I have even heard from our Grigory, who sweeps the floor and almost always talks to himself, that there will soon be a wedding because papa is set on seeing Sophie married to a general or a kammer-junker or a colonel in the army. . . ."

Deuce take it! I can't read any more. . . . It's always a kammer-junker or a general. Everything that's best in the world falls to the kammer-junkers or the generals. If you find some poor treasure and think it is almost within your grasp, a kammer-junker or a general will snatch it from you. The devil take it! I should like to become a general myself, not in order to receive her hand and all the rest of it; no, I should like to be a general only to see how they would wriggle and display all their court manners and *équivoques* and then to say to them: I spit on you both. Deuce take it, it's annoying! I tore the silly dog's letters to bits.

*December* 3.

It cannot be. It's idle talk! There won't be a wedding! What if he *is* a kammer-junker? Why, that is nothing but a dignity, it's not a visible thing that one could pick up in one's hands. You don't get a third eye in your head because you are a kammer-junker. Why, his nose is not made of gold but is just like mine and every one else's; he sniffs with it and doesn't eat with it, he sneezes with it and doesn't cough with it. I have often tried to make out what all these differences come from. Why am I a titular councillor and on what grounds am I a titular councillor? Perhaps I am not a titular councillor at all? Perhaps I am a count or a general, and only somehow appear to be a titular councillor. Perhaps I don't know myself who I am. How many instances there have been in history: some simple, humble tradesman or peasant, not even a nobleman, is suddenly discovered to be a grand gentleman or a baron, or what do you call it. . . . If a peasant can sometimes turn into something like that, what may not a nobleman turn into? I shall suddenly, for instance, go to see our chief in a general's uniform: with an epaulette on my right shoulder and an epaulette on my left shoulder, and a blue ribbon across my chest; well, my charmer will sing a different tune then, and what will her papa, our director, himself say? Ah, he is very ambitious! He is a Mason, he is certainly a Mason; though he does pretend to be this and that, but I noticed at once that he was a Mason: if he shakes hands with any one, he only offers him two fingers. Might I not be appointed a governor-general this very minute or an intendant, or something of that sort? I should like to know why I am a titular councillor. Why precisely a titular councillor?

# A MADMAN'S DIARY

I spent the whole morning reading the newspaper. Strange things are going on in Spain. In fact, I can't really make it out. They write that the throne is vacant, and that they are in a difficult position about choosing an heir, and that there are insurrections in consequence. It seems to me that it is extremely queer. How can the throne be vacant? They say that some Donna ought to ascend the throne. A Donna cannot ascend the throne, she cannot possibly. There ought to be a king on the throne. "But," they say, "there is not a king." It cannot be that there is no king. A kingdom can't exist without a king. There is a king, only probably he is in hiding somewhere. He may be there, but either family reasons or danger from some neighboring State, such as France or some other country, may compel him to remain in hiding, or there may be some other reasons.

December 8.

I quite wanted to go to the department, but various reasons and considerations detained me. I cannot get the affairs of Spain out of my head. How can it be that a Donna should be made queen? They won't allow it. England in the first place won't allow it. And besides, the politics of all Europe, the Emperor of Austria and our Tsar. . . . I must own these events have so overwhelmed and shaken me that I haven't been able to do anything all day. Mavra remarked that I was extremely absent-minded at table. And I believe I did accidentally throw two plates on the floor, which smashed immediately. After dinner I went for a walk down the hill: I could deduce nothing edifying from that. For the most part I lay on my bed and reflected on the affairs of Spain.

2000 A. D., *April* 43.

This is the day of the greatest public rejoicing! There is a king of Spain! He has been discovered. I am that king. I only heard of it this morning. I must own it burst upon me like a flash of lightning. I can't imagine how I could believe and imagine myself to be a titular councillor. How could that crazy, mad idea ever have entered my head? It's a good thing that no one thought of putting me in a madhouse. Now everything has been revealed to me. Now it is all as plain as possible. But until now I did not understand, everything was in a sort of mist. And I believe it all arose from believing that the brain is in the head. It's not so at all; it comes with the wind from the direction of the Caspian Sea. First of all, I told Mavra who I am. When she heard that the King of Spain was standing before her, she clasped her hands and almost died of horror; the silly woman had never seen a king of Spain before. I tried to reassure her, however, and in gracious words tried to convince her of my benevolent feelings towards her, saying that I was not angry with her for having sometimes cleaned my boots so badly. Of course they are benighted people; it is no good talking of elevated subjects to them. She is frightened because she is convinced that all kings of Spain are like Philip II. But I assured her that there was no resemblance between me and Philip II and that I have not even one Capucin. I didn't go to the department. The devil take it! No, my friends, you won't allure me there again; I am not going to copy your nasty papers!

---

# A MADMAN'S DIARY

*Martober* 86 *between day and night.*

Our office messenger arrived to-day to tell me to go to the department, and to say that I had not been there for more than three weeks.

But people are unjust: they do their reckoning by weeks. It's the Jews brought that in because their Rabbi washes once a week. However, I did go to the department for fun. The head of our section thought that I should bow to him and apologize, but I looked at him indifferently, not too angrily and not too graciously, and sat down in my place as though I did not notice anything. I looked at all the scum of the office and thought: "If only you knew who is sitting among you!" Good gracious! wouldn't there be an upset! And the head of our section would bow to me as he bows now to the director. They put a paper before me to make some sort of an extract from it. But I didn't touch it. A few minutes later every one was in a bustle. They said the director was coming. A number of the clerks ran forward to show off to him, but I didn't stir. When he walked through our room they all buttoned up their coats, but I didn't do anything at all. What's a director? Am I going to tremble before him—never! He's a fine director! He is a cork, he is not a director. An ordinary cork, a simple cork and nothing else—such as you cork a bottle with. What amused me most of all was when they put a paper before me to sign. They thought I should write at the bottom of the paper, So-and-so, headclerk of the table—how else should it be! But in the most important place, where the director of the department signs his name, I wrote "Ferdinand VIII." You should have seen the awe-struck silence that followed; but I only waved my hand and said: "I don't insist on any signs of allegiance!" and walked out. From there I walked straight to the director's. He was not at home. The footman did not want to let me in, but I spoke to him in such a way that he let his hands drop. I went straight to her dressing-room. She was sitting before the looking-glass; she jumped up and stepped back on seeing me. I did not tell her that I was the King of Spain, however; I only told her that there was a happiness awaiting her such as she could not imagine, and that in spite of the wiles of our enemies we should be together. I didn't care to say more and walked out. Oh, woman is a treacherous creature! I have discovered now what women are. Hitherto no one has found out with whom woman is in love: I have been the first to discover it. Woman is in love with the devil. Yes, joking apart. Scientific men write nonsense saying that she is this or that—she cares for nothing but the devil. You will see her from a box in the first tier fixing her lorgnette. You imagine she is looking at the fat man with decorations. No, she is looking at the devil who is standing behind his back. There he is, hidden in his coat. There he is, making signs to her! And she will marry him, she will marry him. And all these people, their dignified fathers who fawn on everybody and push their way to court and say that they are patriots and one thing and another: profit, profit is all that these patriots want! They would sell their father and their mother and God for money, ambitious creatures, Judases! All this is ambition, and the ambition is because of a little pimple under the tongue and in it a little worm no bigger than a pin's head, and it's all the doing of a barber who lives in Gorohovy Street, I don't remember his name; but I know for a fact that, in collusion with a midwife, he is trying to spread Mahometanism all over the world, and that is how it is, I am told, that the majority of people in France profess the Mahometan faith.

---

*No date. The day had no number.*

I walked incognito along the Nevsky Prospect. His Majesty the Tsar drove by. All the people took off their caps and I did the same, but I made no sign that I was the King of Spain. I thought it improper to discover myself so suddenly before every one, because I ought first to be presented at court. The only thing that has prevented my doing so is the lack of a Spanish national dress. If only I could get hold of a royal mantle. I should have liked to order it from a tailor, but they are perfect asses; besides they neglect their work so, they have given themselves up to speculating and for the most part are employed in laying the pavement in the street. I determined to make the mantle out of my new uniform, which I had only worn twice. And that the scoundrels should not ruin it I decided to make it myself, shutting the door that no one might see me at it. I ripped it all up with the scissors because the cut has to be completely different.

*I don't remember the date.*
*There was no month either.*
*Goodness knows what to make of it.*

The mantle is completely finished. Mavra gave a shriek when she saw me in it. However, I can't make up my mind to present myself at court, for so far there is no deputation from Spain. It wouldn't be proper to go without deputies: there would be nothing to give weight to my dignity. I expect them from hour to hour.

# A MADMAN'S DIARY

*The 1st.*

I am extremely surprised at the tardiness of the deputies. What can be detaining them? Can it be the machinations of France? Yes, that is the most malignant of States. I went to inquire at the post office whether the Spanish deputies had not arrived; but the postmaster was excessively stupid and knew nothing. "No," he said, "there are no deputies here, but if you care to write a letter I will send it off in accordance with the regulations." Dash it all, what's the use of a letter? A letter is nonsense. Letters are written by chemists, and even then they have to moisten their tongues with vinegar or else their faces would be all over scabs.

MADRID, *February thirtieth.*

And so here I am in Spain, and it happened so quickly that I can hardly realize it yet. This morning the Spanish deputies arrived and I got into a carriage with them. The extraordinary rapidity of our journey struck me as strange. We went at such a rate that within half an hour we had reached the frontiers of Spain. But of course now there are railroads all over Europe, and steamers go very rapidly. Spain is a strange land! When we went into the first room I saw a number of people with shaven heads. I guessed at once that these were either grandees or soldiers because they do shave their heads. I thought the behavior of the High Chancellor, who led me by the hand, extremely strange. He thrust me into a little room and said: "Sit there, and if you persist in calling yourself King Ferdinand, I'll knock the inclination out of you." But knowing that this was only to try me I answered in the negative, whereupon the Chancellor hit me twice on the back with the stick and it hurt so that I almost cried out, but I restrained myself, remembering that this is the custom of chivalry on receiving any exalted dignity, for customs of chivalry persist in Spain to this day. When I was alone I decided to occupy myself with the affairs of state. I discovered that Spain and China are one and the same country, and it is only through ignorance that they are considered to be different kingdoms. I recommend every one to try and write Spain on a bit of paper and it will always turn out China. But I was particularly distressed by an event which will take place to-morrow. To-morrow at seven o'clock a strange phenomenon will occur: the earth will fall on the moon. The celebrated English chemist Wellington has written about it. I must confess that I experience a tremor at my heart when I reflect on the extreme softness and fragility of the moon. You see the moon is generally made in Hamburg, and very badly made too. I am surprised that England hasn't taken notice of it. It was made by a lame cooper, and it is evident that the fool had no idea what a moon should be. He put in tarred cord and one part of olive oil; and that is why there is such a fearful stench all over the world that one has to stop up one's nose. And that's how it is that the moon is such a soft globe that man cannot live on it and that nothing lives there but noses. And it is for that very reason that we can't see our noses, because they are all in the moon. And when I reflected that the earth is a heavy body and when it falls may grind our noses to powder, I was overcome by such uneasiness that, putting on my shoes and stockings, I hastened to the hall of the Imperial Council to give orders to the police not to allow the earth to fall on the moon. The grandees with shaven heads whom I found in great numbers in the hall of the

# A MADMAN'S DIARY

Imperial Council were very intelligent people, and when I said: "Gentlemen, let us save the moon, for the earth is trying to fall upon it!" they all rushed to carry out my sovereign wishes, and several climbed up the walls to try and get at the moon; but at that moment the High Chancellor walked in. Seeing him they all ran in different directions. I as King remained alone. But, to my amazement, the Chancellor struck me with his stick and drove me back to my room! So great is the power of national customs in Spain.

*January of the same year*
(*it came after February*).

So far I have not been able to make out what sort of a country Spain is. The national traditions and the customs of the court are quite extraordinary. I can't make it out, I can't make it out, I absolutely can't make it out. To-day they shaved my head, although I shouted at the top of my voice that I didn't want to become a monk. But I can't even remember what happened afterwards when they poured cold water on my head. I have never endured such hell. I was almost going frantic so that they had a difficulty in holding me. I cannot understand the meaning of this strange custom. It's a stupid, senseless practice! The lack of good sense in the kings who have not abolished it to this day is beyond my comprehension. Judging from all the circumstances, I wonder whether I have not fallen into the hands of the Inquisition, and whether the man I took to be the Grand Chancellor isn't the Grand Inquisitor. Only I cannot understand how a king can be subject to the Inquisition. It can only be through the influence of France, especially of Polignac. Oh, that beast of a Polignac! He has sworn to me enmity to the death. And

---

he pursues me and pursues me; but I know, my friend, that you are the tool of England. The English are great politicians. They poke their noses into everything. All the world knows that when England takes a pinch of snuff, France sneezes.

*The twenty-fifth.*

To-day the Grand Inquisitor came into my room again, but hearing his steps in the distance I hid under a chair. Seeing I wasn't there, he began calling me. At first he shouted "Popristchin!" I didn't say a word. Then: "Aksenty Ivanov! Titular councillor! nobleman!" I still remained silent. "Ferdinand VIII, King of Spain!" I was on the point of sticking out my head, but then I thought: "No, my friend, you won't take me in, I know you: you will be pouring cold water on my head again." However, he caught sight of me and drove me from under the chair with a stick. That damned stick does hurt. However, I was rewarded for all this by the discovery I made to-day. I found out that every cock has a Spain, that it is under his wings not far from his tail.

The Grand Inquisitor went away, however, very wroth, threatening me with some punishment. But I disdain his impotent malice, knowing that he is simply an instrument, a tool of England.

34 ⅃ɘqɯɒʋ⅄ *Yrae* 349.

No, I haven't the strength to endure more. My God! the things they are doing to me! They pour cold water on my head! They won't listen to me, they won't see me, they won't hear me. What have I

done to them? Why do they torture me? What do they want of a poor creature like me? What can I give them? I have nothing. It's too much for me, I can't endure these agonies, my head is burning and everything is going round. Save me, take me away! Give me a troika and horses swift as a whirlwind! Take your seat, my driver, ring out, my bells, fly upwards, my steeds, and bear me away from this world! Far away, far away, so that nothing can be seen, nothing. Yonder the sky whirls before me, a star sparkles in the distance; the forest floats by with dark trees and the moon; blue-grey mist lies stretched under my feet; a chord resounds in the mist; on one side the sea, on the other Italy, yonder the huts of Russia can be seen. Is that my home in the distance? Is it my mother sitting before the window? Mother, save your poor son! Drop a tear on his sick head! See how they torment him! Press your poor orphan to your bosom! There is nowhere in the world for him! he is persecuted! Mother, have pity on your sick child! . . .

And do you know that the Bey of Algiers has a boil just under his nose?